C000149326

# From Manchester to the Arctic

Nurse Sanders embarks on an
adventure that will change her life

Sheena Billett

Copyright © [2022] by Sheena Billett]

All rights reserved.

No portion of this book may be reproduced in any form without written permission from the publisher or author, except as permitted by U.K. copyright law.

Cover design by Kostis Pavlou

To my wife, Glen, without whom this book would never have been written. Thank you for all your memories and your unstinting encouragement and patience when the going got tough.

# Also by Sheena:

**Shifting Horizons:**
A collection of short stories and flash fiction

**Noels'Garden:**
A short story included in **Evergreen (an anthology).** Bridge
House Publishing

"Only those who risk going too far can possibly find out how far they can go." T.S. Eliot

# Foreword

This book is based on the journals and memories of my wife, Glen, who was that impulsive and romantic twenty-one-year-old nurse. During her two years in Arctic Canada, she kept notes and journals which have formed much of the setting for this story. Although Connie, the main character, is loosely based on Glen, she is a fictional creation and her story is just that, a story. All of the other characters are also entirely fictional, as is the setting of Harbour Inlet, so any perceived similarities with people from that time are purely coincidental.

It is important to note here that during the 1970s the Inuit were generally known as 'Eskimos', both in Canada and in the UK, but writing in 2022 it seemed inappropriate to use that term, so I have used the word 'Inuit' to describe Ilannaq and her people in this book.

I have tried to make the content as historically accurate as possible, and Glen's notes from the time have been invaluable, but if any inaccuracies have crept in, I take full responsibility for them.

# Chapter One

The advert in the Situations Vacant column had simply said: *Wanted. Nurses with a sense of adventure.*

Squashed into the red and white Twin Otter floatplane alongside medical supplies, many blue bags and large quantities of alcohol, Connie felt strangely insignificant as she watched the vast white, blue and turquoise Arctic landscape unfold outside the small window. The emptiness was at the same time both thrilling and unnerving. There were no trees, no roads, no cars, no movement, no signs of the busy urban environment she had left behind. It was a blank white page, as yet unspoilt.

There was a tense silence as the pilot searched for a suitable stretch of water for landing. Several times, Connie had been about to breathe again as safety had seemed imminent, only to find herself firmly hauled back up into the air as the pilot aborted the landing at the last minute, the ice floes stubbornly refusing to keep the expanse of water clear for the Otter to land. Feeling that she was trapped in some kind of recurring nightmare, Connie gripped the edge of the seat as the roller coaster ride continued. She firmly tamped down any sense of panic, wondering if she had inherited her grandfather's wandering spirit. Although she had never met him, Frederick James Sanders had been a merchant seaman who had travelled the world, coming home only for brief visits, to ply his family with strange gifts bought in exotic places, and providing his long-suffering wife with yet another mouth to feed in his absence. In her more romantic moments, though, Connie liked to think that maybe she was made of the same stuff as her grandfather and maybe even the great explorers. Harbour Inlet, Baffin Island, the North-West Territories of Canada – she imagined him nodding in satisfaction, from beyond the grave, at her adventurous spirit. According to Connie's father who had not had fond memories of his largely absent parent, he had died a lonely death, apparently, as remote and uncommunicative as ever and had not been missed by his nearest and dearest, in spite of the gifts. She felt a twinge of disloyal sympathy for her fellow traveller.

Connie's departure had happened rapidly. Following an interview at Canada House, in Manchester, and once confirmation of her posting and her visa had come through, there had been little else to do but pack and go. She hadn't felt any regret about leaving home and friends – in fact she hadn't felt much of anything except an all-consuming need to get away from the overwhelming struggle her life had become. At twenty-one Connie felt deep down that she hadn't changed much since leaving school, for ever destined to be on the outside looking in, never part of the gang, always acting up in order to be noticed and accepted. But Helen...Helen had offered hope, had given her a glimpse of something different, had made her feel like she was the only one in the world that mattered, for six exhilarating months. And so her brutal rejection and betrayal had been a sledgehammer, causing Connie's fragile sense of herself to shatter. She had fled, vowing to somehow put all those broken pieces into a box and firmly close the lid. She would never go back there.

Connie's bewildered parents and her brother, David, had taken her to Manchester airport on a dull and cloudy day at the beginning of June1970. The goodbyes had been tense, and although Connie had sensed her parents' upset and disappointment, she hadn't been able to conceal her desperation to get away from them as soon as they'd arrived at the terminal. Consumed by thoughts of the Arctic, she'd worn a thick, brown woollen trouser suit, which, in the event, proved exactly the wrong thing to be wearing when she arrived in Montreal's sizzling Canadian summer heat – the temperature hovering at around ninety degrees.

After a one-night stopover, the first time she had ever slept in another country – her only other foreign excursion being a day trip to Paris with some nursing friends, where they had all drunk too much and returned the worse for wear late that evening – Connie had found herself, the next morning on a plane to Frobisher Bay, and for the first time became aware that Canada wasn't the English-speaking country that she'd naïvely imagined. She could make out snippets of French reminding her of terrifying French lessons at school, from where a dim memory surfaced that many Canadians were indeed French-speaking. But alongside the French was something composed of sounds that Connie had never experienced before. The speakers of this unfamiliar language were Inuit, most of whom Connie assumed were travelling home to Frobisher Bay and maybe on to settlements beyond. In this swirl of other tongues, Connie had felt the first uncomfortable stirrings of anxiety now beginning to mingle with the desperation to escape that had brought her, unthinking, to this point.

Frobisher Bay was the largest settlement on Baffin Island. A growing frontier town, with all the benefits of a major hub, including an airport – with regular flights to and from Montreal, a modern hospital, schools (both Catholic and Protestant) and a large store which was the main hub for the Hudson Bay Company. Intended as only a brief stopover, in the end it had been home Connie for two interminable weeks, while she had waited for weather conditions to be right for a flight to Harbour Inlet. She spent the time aimlessly wandering around, impatient to get to her destination and start her new life. She found that bars and dance halls were plentiful, and learnt on her hastily arranged training days at the hospital that Westerners had already brought with them the plagues of alcoholism and STDs to a people not equipped to cope with either.

When no flight seemed imminent, one of the sisters at the hospital suggested that Connie use the time to have some further training and meet colleagues who, she assured Connie, would become distant lifelines over the next year or so. Although impatient to get to Harbour Inlet, Connie was glad to learn more about her work. It seemed that much of her time would be spent combatting the plague of TB that was rampaging through the Inuit communities. She would be responsible for persuading the Inuit community in and around Harbour Inlet to get tested and vaccinated, and for spotting any suspected cases – which would need to be sent to the TB clinic in Frobisher Bay without delay. Connie was daunted as the realisation dawned that she, and she alone would also have to deal with any other medical emergencies that arose, and so was grateful for a few days on the maternity ward, revisiting her midwifery skills, as well as time in the Emergency Unit, revising her first aid and stitching. She was relieved to see that the techniques were much the same as she had been trained to use back in Manchester.

In a bizarre twist of fate, the Queen and Prince Phillip has chosen the same time to visit this far-flung outpost of her empire with Prince Charles and Princess Anne, and the excitement and brief glimpse of the motorcade, had been strangely comforting – a glimpse of home in a far-flung city. Connie had waved and cheered with much more enthusiasm than she would done have at home, where the royal family had seemed a distant entity, far from the life she knew. But here they were a link with something familiar, and Connie felt a strange sense of loss when they inevitably moved on to their next destination, leaving her behind.

In the evenings Connie listened to the unearthly creaks and groans of huge blocks of ice grinding and crashing together in the bay, as the sea melted and tides came and went. Haunting sounds that she would never forget, along with the annual break-up sight and smell of rotting seal, walrus, husky and other, unidentifiable carcasses that washed ashore.

She went to the cinema a few times, a place of comforting familiarity, never getting over the novelty of the late-night daylight when she came out of the darkness, and the sounds of children playing in the middle of the night, as she tried to sleep. It was hard to get used to a way of life that was not dominated by the clock or the 'pips' on the radio. The Inuit had no such restrictions.

As the days passed with no news of a flight, Connie began to wonder if she would ever get to her destination. She looked longingly out over the ice floes from her hotel room, praying for something to happen before she lost her nerve or ran out of money, and booked a flight home.

Eventually she learnt that the Hudson Bay manager in Frobisher Bay had been on an inspection visit to their store in Harbour Inlet, taking advantage of an emergency flight to evacuate a young woman with a retained placenta. A risky return flight had been arranged to take various provisions, and Connie jumped at the chance to grab the only passenger seat on the plane in spite of having been warned by the pilot that landing would be likely be precarious as he would have to find a large enough expanse of water between the ice floes. As this was break-up time, the ice was too weak to bear the weight of a fully loaded plane and the sand bars had not yet formed to allow a more traditional landing. Connie was to soon learn that any kind of Arctic travel involved some kind of weather-related risk.

Eventually, seizing the moment, and with expert handling the pilot deftly took possession of a stretch of ice-blue water, and after a precarious landing, Connie was ready for whatever the Arctic had to offer. She was vaguely aware of the clicking of a camera noting every move of her unceremonious transfer to a seemingly flimsy canoe, already full of Inuit paddlers. A second canoe received the blue bags, alcohol and her medical supplies from the pilot of the Otter. Waving goodbye to him, Connie turned and smiled uncertainly at her new acquaintances.

The rhythmic motion of the silent paddlers carried her, with a sense of inevitability, to her new life as she heard the Otter take off behind her. There was no turning back now, and Connie gripped the sides of the canoe, her heart beating and her hands sweating. As they neared the shore she became aware of a small group awaiting their arrival, and feeling a growing sense of dread, she willed herself to keep calm as the Inuit rowers skilfully beached the canoe.

Once she had disembarked, with slightly more grace, a tall grey-haired man strode forward and shook Connie's hand. 'Welcome to Harbour Inlet.' He gave her a brisk handshake. From the corner of her eye, she saw the blue bags, crates of alcohol, and her luggage, being briskly conveyed by the paddlers to where a white man, hands on hips, was waiting impatiently further up the beach. There were rapid exchanges in Inuktitut and Connie wondered how she would ever understand anything in this alien tongue. More unwelcome memories of humiliation in French lessons at school surged into her mind, recollections of how incompatible French pronunciation had seemed with her Manchester accent.

The grey-haired man turned to Connie and introduced himself as, Reverend Brooks, Church of England Vicar. He then introduced Connie to other members of the community who had suddenly appeared. Word of her arrival had spread surprisingly quickly, it seemed.

'This is Jim Briggs, the Hudson Bay Company manager.' A round, fat and surprisingly effeminate man for a fur trader stepped forward to shake her hand. Connie's gaze was drawn to his tiny feet. While endlessly waiting for her flight from Frobisher Bay, Connie had read about the all-encompassing, power of the Hudson Bay influence in the area and had vague knowledge about their fur-trading business with the locals.

'Great to meet you. I'm sure you'll liven us all up in no time.' Connie noticed that the main focus of his attention, however, was the crates of beer and whisky, currently being stacked onto a small trolley.

Rev Brooks gave him a stern look and turned to a middle-aged couple. 'This is Thierry Banning and his wife, Françoise. Thierry is our engineer – we're totally dependent on him if anything breaks down.' Like Jim, Thierry's attention was drawn to the now-stacked whisky and beer, only giving Connie a brief nod of welcome.

'*Bonjour*, Connie.' Françoise stepped forward and gave Connie a hug.

'And this is our assistant administrator, Peter.'

Connie noticed the expensive-looking camera slung around Peter's neck. 'Was that you taking the photos back there?'

'Yes, indeed. Peter is our resident photographer.' Rev Brooks answered for him, as Peter stepped forward and shook Connie's hand warmly. 'Welcome to Harbour Inlet, Connie.'

'And this is my wife.' It seemed that Mrs Brooks was almost an afterthought, as she stepped forward to greet Connie. If she'd had to imagine a vicar's wife, it would be Mrs Brooks, short and stout with her prim, greying bun and rimless spectacles.

Connie was quickly disabused of any notion that the welcoming party was purely for her benefit, as increasingly, all eyes were drawn to the packages and blue bags currently being sorted and checked against a list by the impatient man and an officious-looking RCMP officer.

'There is much excitement as this is the first delivery we've had in over two months. These blue bags contain post and packages from many families and friends.' The focus of even Rev Brooks's eyes was starting to drift towards the enticing blue bags. 'Come and meet Paul Archer the government administrator for Harbour Inlet,' he said, striding over to where the unloading was almost finished. 'Paul and the RCMP will sort everything out and then distribute it. The supplies you brought with you will be delivered to the Nurse's Station by this evening. Paul deals with all the administration for the Nurse's Station, so you'll need to go through him for supplies. As you can see, he is busy today so I'm afraid you will have to make do with me.'

'Paul, this is Nurse Sanders.'

'Connie, please,' said Connie, holding out her hand.

'Not again! When will they ever learn to stop sending these inexperienced young nurses?' Paul raised his eyes to the sky and let out a frustrated sigh.

Connie quickly withdrew the proffered hand and took a step back. As she did so, one of the Inuit men beckoned Paul over and he walked away without a backward glance.

Rev Brooks ignored Paul's rudeness as if it hadn't happened. 'Right, let me show you where you're going to be living.'

A tingle of real fear and apprehension trickled down Connie's spine as the rest of the small crowd, obviously not deemed important enough to be introduced to Connie, started to disperse towards the blue bags. She noticed a young woman standing apart from the others who gave her a smile and a hesitant wave as she passed. Connie smiled back in what she hoped was a friendly way as she was ushered firmly away by Rev Brooks.

# Chapter Two

O nce Rev Brooks had departed, having given her many bewildering instructions about where things were and how they worked, Connie stood in silence in her first home and suddenly felt very grown-up. She was drawn to the large window at one end of the living room and stood looking out at the ice floes and the open sea beyond. Could she be happy here? Was she up to this adventure which was already morphing into something way beyond anything she had imagined?

The basic shack-like wooden exterior of the hut, belied the modern, well-equipped kitchen, comfortable lounge and well-proportioned bedroom within. Connie felt a tickle of excitement. This was her very own home, to do with as she wished – and she intended to enjoy the experience to the full. Ignoring her mother's stern warnings about the dire consequences of expressing too much emotion, Connie threw out her arms and literally danced with joy. She started as she meant to go on.

Eventually, when everything was unpacked, neatly folded and put away and a few other items she had brought with her were artfully arranged, Connie was sitting and admiring her small empire when she became aware of the sound of firm footsteps echoing around her house. She stood up in alarm, heart pounding.

'I'm Elizabeth. Sorry I wasn't there when you arrived, but I gather you've met my husband, Peter.' Connie noticed the Scottish accent before she registered the speaker, a brisk, athletic looking young woman.

'Oh...hello.' Connie, willing her heart to stop pounding, could think of nothing else to say.

The expression on Elizabeth's face softened. 'I'm so sorry, we shouldn't have barrelled in like that. But around here, most of us don't stand on any formalities, we just walk in and out of each other's houses all the time.'

For the first time, Connie realised that 'we' included a small boy, peeping at her from behind his mother's leg.

'This is Tom.' Elizabeth picked him up in her strong arms as if he weighed hardly anything. 'Say hello to Connie, Tom.'

Tom gave a shy wave.

'I just popped by to say that we're having a bit of a get-to-gether tonight. It would be great if you came, and then you can meet people a bit more...informally.' Elizabeth gave a wry smile. 'I heard about the reception committee earlier.'

Connie relaxed and smiled in return. 'Yes, that would be great, thank you, Elizabeth.'

'See you later then. We're in the Teacher's House above the Nurse's Station.'

It was only after Elizabeth had gone, that Connie realised she hadn't asked her what time she should arrive. Maybe around here it didn't really matter. She felt strangely comforted by the presence of this friendly woman, and instinctively knew that Elizabeth would make this place less lonely.

As she walked toward the Teacher's House, at around 7.30, a time she judged might be suitable, Connie marvelled at the pristine beauty of the vast, empty landscape around her. Becoming increasingly aware of the quiet stillness that was both unnerving and intoxicating after the grime and noise of Manchester. She stood overwhelmed, as only the sound her own breathing stirred the air. This was not the flat, end-less wasteland that she had been imagining. It was a land of majestic, snow-covered mountains, and glaciers that swept down to the sea under an ice-blue sky as remains of forgotten icebergs, brilliant in their aqua-blue coats bobbed about in the ocean waiting their silent and final return to the sea. Connie's heart swelled. She was a romantic at heart and had often been moved to tears at the beauty of mountains, hills, rivers and lakes of Scotland, or a magnificent sunset over the sea, even if she had no one to share the joy with. The Arctic, however, was something completely different and Connie wondered if she would ever get over the awe she felt in this place.

In contrast to the vast landscape around her, when Connie looked down, she saw hundreds of tiny, pink and white flow-ers attached to thick, sturdy plants growing low on the ground on either side of the path. Something she hadn't expected, even in summer, this far north.

The scattered hut-like buildings and shacks gave the set-tlement a temporary, just-discovered feel, and the wooden, unprepossessing church seemed an imposing building in this setting. There was a hall next to the church, which on closer inspection, she saw doubled as a school. By far the largest building, however, was the Hudson Bay trading post which had its own Hudson Bay Store.

Like hers, Elizabeth and Peter's house overlooked the bay and was well-equipped, even luxurious, by English standards. As she entered, Elizabeth rushed forward and gave Connie a warm hug. Her luxuriant dark hair framed an attractive face and her soft brown eyes sparkled a welcome.

By the time they had consumed a few drinks, Connie had regaled them with stories of her travels thus far and was revelling in having an appreciative audience. She was on safe territory here and always knew how to make people laugh.

'Oh my God, you are going to be such a breath of fresh air, Connie,' Elizabeth spluttered between giggles. 'I'm afraid these are the last bits and pieces we have in the way of party food. A supply ship comes once a year to replenish our depleted stocks and to bring building materials or anything else that Harbour Inlet needs. You're in luck – it's due any day now.'

'Well, I think it looks impressive anyway.' Connie eyed the slices of fruit cake, along with some bread and jam, nuts, and biscuits.

A few minutes later, Jim Briggs arrived, closely followed by Thierry and Françoise. As Jim reached for his drink, she noticed once more his small, oddly delicate hands, and as she lifted her head, her gaze was met with a pair of tiny, alert, dark eyes that reminded her of a bird's steady gaze that missed nothing. Thierry, Connie discovered, knew more about the Arctic north than any of the others in the room. He had lived in Harbour Inlet for twenty-five years and had no intention of returning to his native Quebec. Françoise, it seemed, was happy to be wherever Thierry was. She noticed that Jim and Thierry were wasting no time in getting stuck into the newly arrived whisky.

As the evening went on, several others joined the group and Connie found herself realising that these were the people were going to be her world for the foreseeable future and she was going to have to get on with them if life was to be bearable. Tired as she was, she made an effort to join in with various conversations feeling very much an outsider to the in-jokes, inevitable in such an isolated community. The all-too-familiar fear of being on the outside of things started to surface and Connie fought the urge not to flee back to her house – humiliation burning at being side-lined so soon after her arrival. Her rational self sternly reminded her that she shouldn't have expected any other, and that this wasn't personal.

Just as she had got a grip on her panic, Connie's stomach churned as Paul Archer arrived. She shrank into a corner of the settee hoping he wouldn't notice her. But Elizabeth, apparently, had other ideas and ushered him over. 'Paul is your go-to person if you need any additional supplies or have any questions about your work.' Connie's heart sank at the thought that she might have to deal with this man on a day-to-day basis.

'We've met.' Paul was already turning away when Elizabeth turned to deal with Tom who was pulling on her trouser leg.

'I'll leave you to it.' Elizabeth left Paul with little choice but to turn back to Connie.

'You don't look old enough to be a nurse. How long have you been qualified?' Paul looked down on her.

'Only a few months.'

Paul gave an explosive sigh, making Connie jump, although she tried to hide it. 'What on earth were they thinking sending someone with no experience for this job...again! I guarantee you won't last more than a few months, just like your predecessor. You'll probably be on the flight back to Frobisher Bay at the end of the summer – along with Elizabeth and Peter.'

Before Connie could answer, Jim and Thierry approached. 'Come on, Paul, you're wasting valuable drinking time!' They both gave Connie a cursory nod – Jim's slightly more lingering before returning to their positions next to the whisky.

'I'll bet this is a bit different to Manchester.' Elizabeth reappeared at Connie's side.

Connie was getting over her shock that Elizabeth would only be a temporary friend and didn't really register her question. When it became apparent that a response was required, Connie pulled herself together. 'Yes, but it's going to be amazing to enjoy learning new things and meeting new people,' Connie said without, at that moment, believing it. 'Is it true that you are only here until the end of the summer?' The question was out before Connie could stop herself. Somehow, in her terror she felt herself clinging on to this woman like a life raft after a shipwreck. How ridiculous was that?

Elizabeth looked at her fondly, almost as if she could read Connie's mind. 'Yes, we're only here while the teachers, Kathy and Tom, are on their summer break. But don't worry, by then you'll have met everyone and made new friends. You'll do it. You'll survive, I can sense it.'

Connie felt close to tears and needed to escape to cry in the privacy of her own house. 'Sorry, Elizabeth, I'm exhausted, but thank you – thank you so much.'

'It was a pleasure, and you're welcome here any time,' Elizabeth said as she placed an arm around Connie's shoulder, kissing her gently on the cheek. 'Don't let Paul get to you, he's like this with anyone new, especially women.' But Connie was not reassured. Had she come all this way to be bullied and belittled all over again?

# Chapter Three

It was almost 3 a.m. before Connie got into bed. Sipping cocoa in the cold daylight and listening to the silence, only punctuated by the distant barking of dogs, she began to wonder what she had done. What if she had made a disastrous mistake? She had almost convinced herself that she would have to return home in disgrace, having failed as an explorer and adventurer at the first hurdle. But then she remembered Elizabeth's final words: 'You can do it, I can tell.' She thought of her grandfather again and some deep sense of determination kicked in, and Connie knew that she was not going to fail without giving it all she had. She'd signed up for an adventure and now she was bloody well going to have one!

After a fitful sleep, Connie arose to a day of a completely new kind. The sun was still in the sky, but today she had to sort out her work routine. She found that she was not as fazed by this prospect as she had been about meeting so many people last night. Getting ready, Connie discovered that the luxuries of home were not as readily available, and she had yet to learn the strange ways of the oil heating and her Aga cooker. She knew that the settlement had its own generator for electricity, but heating and cooking appliances relied mainly on oil – which like everything else, was delivered annually and carefully rationed. Connie was grateful for the warmth of the Aga next to her bedroom, and understood why there were no internal doors, as the warm air circulated around her house. Rev Davies, among his many instructions had warned Connie to use water sparingly as it was delivered to the tank in her house twice a week by Innik who travelled to a freshwater lake, locally known as Cooper's Pond, around a mile or so from the settlement, to pump water into a huge tanker-type vehicle on skis in the winter and wheels in the summer, which he then brought overland and delivered water to each household. She had noticed the day before that each house had a large storage tank on the inner porch. It seemed ironic to Connie that, although for much of the year they would be surrounded by snow and ice, fresh water was a valuable commodity.

Connie had also learnt that the mains sewage system she had taken for granted at home, did not exist in Harbour Inlet – this was something she had not even thought about! There was not a flush toilet to be had, but rather, a rudimentary tin can, complete with lid and a mysterious black plastic bag. Innik, as well as delivering the water, also collected these 'honey buckets' twice a week – but on a different day to the water delivery Connie was pleased to learn. What happened to the contents of these honey buckets was something of a mystery, although Connie already knew enough to be aware that the solid permafrost didn't allow for any digging for easy disposal. Connie decided that she didn't need to know any more about the unsavoury details of sewage disposal and turned her mind to other things.

She decided, as it was summer, not to dress, as she had been shown in Frobisher Bay, and to discard the layer of thermals, which, she had been told would become like a second skin, especially though the long winter months. She did, however, put on a thick, woollen sweater. Even though the temperature was a couple of degrees above freezing, Connie was taking no chances – she might be spending a lot of time in unheated conditions today. Connie was also realising that when the winter temperatures kicked in, she would need to allow quite a bit of time to get dressed – and undressed again – at the end of the day! Gone were the days of throwing on her uniform in a few minutes after a night out and arriving on the ward just in time to avoid Sister's icy disapproval.

Connie fortified herself for the day ahead with coffee and a round or two of unappetising toast. Elizabeth had told her that the butter came in tins on the yearly visit of the supply ship – and this, being last year's supply, had a decidedly rancid taste – but it was better than nothing.

She stepped into the inner porch, past a large freezer – and yes it was possible to sell fridges and freezers to inhabitants of the Arctic, it seemed, as they were vital to store the supplies that came on the annual visit of the supply ship. Only essential freight was shipped in by air, apparently. Connie thought ruefully back to the crates of beer and whisky that had accompanied her on yesterday's flight. Maybe, here, 'essentials' were different than back at home. Also, in the inner porch, there were yet more layers to put on, this time in the form of two pairs of thick socks, and sealskin boots known as *kamiks*. She had come across these in Montreal but had never handled them. Now, examining the inner layer of duffel, and the brightly patterned outer layer of sealskin, Connie marvelled at the intricate and skilled stitching required for such detailed decoration, and putting them on, she was amazed at how light they were – so different from the clumpy, leather shoes at home.

Heading for the Nurse's Centre, situated in the basement of the Teachers' House, Connie retraced her steps from the previous evening, sure that this would become a well-trodden path. She noticed there were a number of Inuit dwellings in

Harbour Inlet. These were mainly shacks that had an impermanent feel about them and appeared to have been hurriedly constructed out of driftwood and odd pieces of galvanised metal – whatever had been at hand, she guessed. Many had wooden racks at the front where various skins had been hung to dry. On closer examination, Connie saw that these frames had been cleverly designed to stretch as well as dry the pelts. Several huskies were tethered to posts around a few of the dwellings. She had heard them barking in the ever-present daylight of the previous night.

Connie did what came naturally to her and approached one of the dogs, her hand stretched out in welcome, but jumped hastily back as the dog lunged and bared its teeth. An elderly Inuit woman shouted from the doorway of a nearby hut, and when Connie turned, she shook her head disapprovingly. Suitably chastened, Connie continued on her way. The settlement appeared to be busy with Inuit coming to trade at the Hudson Bay depot, and a few other Westerners who Connie didn't recognise.

Expectations which had already been dropping by the hour, hit an all-time low at the sight of the Nurse's Station. Connie knew that much of her work involved treating and vaccinating the local Inuit settlements for TB, but nothing, however, had prepared her for the sparsity of the 'Nurse's Station'. She saw that the TB treatments and the few other medications that she had brought from Frobisher Bay had been piled against one wall, but apart from that, the room contained a bed, desk and chair, and a cabinet, which on inspection contained only some basic medicines and a first-aid kit. Bearing in mind that the nearest hospital was over two hundred miles away in Frobisher Bay and that doctors had to be contacted via radio telephone, Connie felt that medical provisions were somewhat limited. Of more concern, Connie thought as she sorted the stock, was the fact that she had been trained to give nursing care, and felt her knowledge of diagnostics was vague, to say the least! She realised that she was going to have to be doctor, nurse, dentist, and psychiatrist to this isolated community, as well as tackling the appalling lack of any health and welfare programme for the Inuit community. A sense of adventure, yes, but not the kind of Enid Blyton adventure Connie had vaguely imagined – this was real life and death stuff with real people. Connie felt herself growing up fast.

She was engrossed in the finer points of surgical dressings when a young, short and sturdy Inuit woman appeared in the doorway. Assuming this might be her very first patient, Connie jumped up.

'Hello. What can I do for you?'

Connie was surprised when her visitor gave a wide grin before answering in perfect English. 'Hello, Nurse Sanders? I'm your interpreter, Ilannaq. I'll go with you when you visit the settlements. I'm sorry I wasn't here to meet you yesterday.'

Connie's relief was immense. She had been increasingly worried about communicating with her patients in spite of the reassurances at Frobisher Bay that an interpreter would be on hand. Most of the Inuit in Harbour Inlet spoke a little, basic, English, but she knew that wouldn't be the case further afield and she wondered how capable the interpreter might be. Her relief that her help had appeared in the form of this friendly Inuit woman and not another Paul Archer almost brought tears to her eyes.

'Oh, hello, Ilannaq. I'm so pleased to meet you. And call me Connie.' Connie wasn't sure of Inuit etiquette but shook Ilannaq's hand warmly anyway. Ilannaq's animated smile lit up her round face.

'I worked with Pam, who was here before you, although I don't think she was very happy,' Ilannaq said, shaking her head. 'I think we were too much for her.' There was an unmistakeable twinkle in Ilannaq's eye. 'I'm glad the *kamiks* fit. I had to guess your size, but you can always wear more or fewer socks as required.'

'They're beautiful. Who made them?'

'My mother. She is an excellent sewer and we thought they would make a good welcome present.' Ilannaq smiled her wide smile again.

Well, I'm staying, now whatever happens. I wouldn't want to disappoint your mother.' Connie spoke with much more confidence than she felt, remembering her late-night determination to succeed, come what may. 'So when do we start? I've brought the first batch of vaccines and tests with me.'

'Okay, tomorrow we'll go by boat to visit a settlement not too far from here. There are about twenty adults to be vaccinated, and others to be tested. Pam didn't write anything down, but I can remember who has been vaccinated, and who has already been tested, and when, in here.' Ilannaq pointed to her head, grinning. 'I know all the disc numbers.'

'Disc numbers?' Connie racked her brains. Had anyone mentioned disc numbers?

'They didn't tell you? All of us Inuit have been allocated a disc number by the government, because we don't have...second names, like you. It's a way for them to keep track of us.' She gave a wry smile. 'I am Ilannaq E7-143.'

Connie tried to hide her shock. But the '*What?*' was out of her mouth before she could think.

'How else are we going to keep our records straight?' Ilannaq commented with equanimity.

Connie guessed that was a fair point and knew she would never be comfortable with such a barbaric system, but at the same time made a mental note to make sure her record-keeping would be second-to-none.

'Right, I'll get everything ready. Do you think I'll be able to do some basic health checks while we're there?'

'If they like you, maybe,' said Ilannaq vaguely.

When Ilannaq had gone, Connie returned to her list of requests with renewed vigour, still grappling with alien concepts. When she thought about it, though, maybe it was the equivalent of National Insurance numbers back home. But it still didn't seem right.

Having completed a preliminary survey of her workspace, Connie was at a loss as to what to do next. It wasn't as if there was a queue of patients outside awaiting her attention, so she headed off to the Hudson Bay store to locate the 2-way radio station that she knew would be her umbilical cord to the outside world. Jim was more than happy to show her around and give her a brief introduction to the world of long-distance communication. However, after half an hour of his company Connie was feeling distinctly uncomfortable and there was no mistaking his agenda, betrayed by casual physical contact at every opportunity. Eventually she managed to extricate herself from his clutches and left, thankful that at least Paul Archer hadn't been around.

She was retracing her steps back to the Nurse's Station when the Brooks's door opened and Mrs Brooks called her over, much like the head teacher beckoning her into her office at school – somewhere Connie had gone many times – too many times – before she decided to mend her ways. The house was next to the church and painted in the same grey and yellow uniform. St Paul's mission, as it had originally been called had been founded in 1909, back in the days of real pioneer missionaries, who had inhabited this space with the Inuit along with a few RCMP personnel. Connie had read about this in the sparse introductory material she had been given.

'I saw you over at the store and thought you might be headed in this direction, dear. Come in.'

Connie's first impression of Mrs Brooks from the day before as the archetypal vicar's wife was confirmed. A plump woman, probably in her fifties, she looked a lot older, maybe due to the harsh conditions she had lived in with her missionary husband over the last twenty years in various Inuit settlements. Her almost-white hair was parted down the middle and secured at the nape of her neck in a severe bun. A set of thick, rimless glasses completed the look. She could have been acting a part in an Agatha Christie play. And in spite of the 'dear' in her welcome, Connie felt that she was being sized up, and inevitably found wanting – a feeling all too familiar.

'Come in, come in,' she said. 'We were just about to have our morning cocoa.'

And Connie stepped from the Arctic north straight into a middle-class home-counties sitting room complete with chintz settees, a piano, several bookcases, and a patterned carpet. She became aware of a side table set for 'elevenses' with violet-covered china cups and saucers, and a plate set out with exactly three biscuits.

'Good morning, Nurse Sanders.' She jumped as Rev Brooks uncoiled himself from a large armchair in the corner. 'I was just listening to the BBC World Service, they're broadcasting the cricket from Lords.' Only the view from the window betrayed the true location of this home-from-home room.

Connie sat with Rev and Mrs Brooks at the table, which had been placed for easy viewing of the main areas of the settlement, complete with an unsettling pair of binoculars on the windowsill, reminding Connie that she had been seen coming away from the Hudson Bay building.

Following Grace – Connie couldn't remember ever having said Grace before a meal – she dutifully consumed her cup of cocoa and the single biscuit.

Following the inevitable questions about 'home' and why she had felt the need to come to the Arctic, the Brooks's were apparently satisfied that God had called Connie to work there – the narrative that fitted their beliefs. There was no way she would ever share anything resembling the truth of her flight with these two.

Just as Mrs Brooks was asking her, 'What do your parents do, dear?' a welcome diversion occurred in the form of the young girl Connie had seen on the edge of the gathering when she had arrived. On closer inspection, Connie guessed that she must be around eleven or twelve, and she immediately recognised herself at that age, all too well – tall, gangly, awkward, and already exuding a feeling of discomfort with who she was - apart from the piercing blue eyes that Esther turned in her direction.

'This is our daughter, Esther.'

Esther shifted uneasily on her feet and gave Connie a faint smile. Connie noticed that she wasn't in turn introduced to Esther. This was a girl who was already used to being ignored, and Connie's heart went out to her. As Esther made a rapid exit, Connie brought her mind back to her earlier concerns about needing medical back-up.

'Rev Brooks, if I'm going to be able to look after the health of this community, I'm going to need some points of contact. There will be times when I'm going to need medical advice. Apart from the doctors and other staff in Frobisher Bay, who are the other nurses, like me – living out in the settlements? I heard something about other nurses when I was in Frobisher Bay but didn't think to ask about details.'

Rev Brooks gave her an appraising look, and...had she detected a hint of approval?

'A good point, as you will need help and support from time to time. And yes, we can give you a list of colleagues in other settlements whose experience will prove invaluable to you. Your predecessor was sadly, out of her depth, and did nothing but give a few TB shots here and there. The Inuit didn't take to her attitude – they knew she didn't really want to be here.'

'She only lasted a few months, and then headed home to Australia.' Mrs Brooks pursed her lips, disapprovingly. 'I gather there was some *boyfriend* at home.'

'Well, you won't have that problem with me,' replied Connie with certain conviction.

'Paul is indeed the man you need, to show you how to contact the other nurses on the 2-Way radio. Although we do have a radio here for emergencies, you'll find it's generally easier to use the Hudson Bay set. I'll arrange a meeting with him tomorrow morning.'

Connie was already dreading her scheduled meeting with Paul, but at least the silver lining was that she wouldn't have to deal with the wandering hands of Jim Briggs.

# Chapter Four

T hat evening, as Connie returned, exhausted to her home, she poured a warming brandy, got undressed and wrapped herself in a thick, lemon-coloured dressing gown. Her mother had made sure that everything Connie had brought was thick and warm, and right now, she was grateful, making a mental note to write to her parents and let them know that she was okay.

Still revelling in the novelty of having her own home, Connie noticed for the first time how bright and clean everything looked, and felt excited at the thought of cooking something in her very own kitchen – although, at this stage, she had no idea what that might be. So far, her culinary skills were limited to brewing coffee – a jug of which she had put on to boil – and making toast. Coffee, she had learnt from Elizabeth, was almost always brewing in Canadian households, and doors were always open to welcome visitors.

Connie looked around her living room. It was comfortable, but she wanted to rearrange the seating so that she was facing the window and could look out over the bay, to see the changes in the landscape as winter approached. The settee was going to require some heavy lifting, and she just beginning to make some changes when a loud knock on the door startled her. Connie scarcely had time to walk across the room before the door burst open and a tall young woman, wearing a brightly coloured parka, thick navy trousers and a red, woollen bobble hat, strode in. Removing her hat to reveal a mop of blonde, curly hair, she said, 'Hi, I was just passing, smelt the coffee and thought I would pop in and say hello.'

Before Connie had a chance to recover herself and speak, her visitor rushed on without a pause. 'I'm Daisy. Oh, and I have a message from Paul. He's asked if you can meet him the day after tomorrow, as he's out of the settlement until then.' Her visitor stopped abruptly, as if noticing Connie for the first time. 'Wow, that's some dressing gown!'

Connie looked down to hide her embarrassment as the gown brushed the floor. 'My mother insisted,' she replied, choosing to laugh off her discomfort. 'Thanks for the message though. I'd forgotten that I'm not going to be here tomorrow either. I'm off to one of the settlements with Ilannaq.' Connie mentally berated herself for her inefficiency. How could she have forgotten that when she'd agreed to the meeting with Paul? She was thankful that fate had intervened and prevented yet another humiliating scene with Paul Archer.

While Connie poured some coffee, Daisy finished introducing herself: 'I work for the Canadian government up here. I'm working on a study of the decline in the culture of the Baffin Island Inuit.'

Connie recognised the Canadian accent.

'Wow! I'm surprised the government is even interested, if their commitment to medical care is anything to go by.'

'I'd be really interested in any input you can give from your nursing perspective.'

'I'd love to take part. But I thought I'd met everyone who was anyone at the get-together last night,' Connie risked a teasing tone.

'Things like that are not my style really, and apart from that I had a lot of work to do. Did you enjoy it?'

As they moved from the kitchen to the living room, Connie was reminded of her plans to reposition the furniture and was wondering if she could ask Daisy to help, when she realised that an answer was required.

'Oh yes, the party... Yes it was okay, and it was so nice of Elizabeth and Peter to go to all that trouble. They seem a really nice couple. I'm not so sure about Paul Archer though.'

'He's had a bad experience with women somewhere along the way, which is why he's ended up here. He used to be in the police, but he never talks about his past or any family. It's a story for another time.'

Connie took the hint and changed the subject. 'How long have you been in Harbour Inlet?'

'I came last winter and have another year to do. It's been tough, but an amazing experience and I'm hoping the research will be worth it in the end.' Daisy talked about how damaging the introduction of Western culture had already been for the Inuit, becoming passionate and angry. Connie warmed to her and liked that she cared so much about her work.

'Take the dog teams, for example: traditionally, each family would have their own team of five or six dogs. If the weather turned bad while they were out hunting, they used the dogs to keep warm, or to find a safe way home. But now we've given them skidoos, and if they break down in the middle of nowhere, you can't cuddle up to them. There are only a few teams left in Harbour Inlet now, although they are still used in the more distant settlements.' Daisy hung her head and looked at the floor. 'And we call that progress!'

'I've seen some of the dogs, but when I tried to approach one of them it nearly bit my hand off – or would have done if it hadn't been tethered.'

Connie was taken aback at Daisy's fit of giggles. Once she had recovered and wiped the tears from her eyes, Connie asked, 'What's so funny?' She was aware of a hard edge in her tone. If there was one thing she couldn't stand, it was being humiliated and made fun of, and some instances she never forgot.

Daisy, apparently oblivious, answered, 'These dogs are not pets, Connie. I know you British are obsessed with keeping animals as pets.' Connie found herself still bristling with anger, not in the mood for teasing. 'The dogs only relate to their owners and no one else can encroach into that relationship. The dogs are part of the Inuit livelihood and are there only as long as they serve a purpose. There is no room for sentimental attachment to animals in this world.'

'So what happens when they are no use?' Connie said in a small voice, her irritation evaporating at the thought of the fate that might be in store for the dog she had reached out to that morning, not even knowing if she wanted to hear the answer.

'If a dog breaks a leg, gets too old, or can't be of use it will be shot and the meat used to feed the other dogs, or even people in an emergency, and the skin used for clothing.'

Connie gasped, her hand over her mouth, tears filling her eyes as she thought of the family Labrador, Jess, who had been a companion all through her childhood.

Daisy gazed out of the window.

Connie changed the subject, glad of an opportunity to get herself together. 'I've heard about other settlement nurses. Do you know any of them, or how I could make contact?'

Daisy turned to look at her. 'Yes, I know Patty, over at Pond Inlet. She and I have a coffee sometimes. And there's Linda. They are both experienced nurses and have been up here for several years. I'm sure they would love to get to know you, and would be more than happy to give advice or help. Would you like me to ask them to get in touch?'

'That would be great, Daisy. Thank you.' Connie couldn't think of anything else to say as weariness suddenly kicked in and she leant back on the settee.

'Oh God, I'd better get going – stuff to do!' Daisy stood suddenly, taking Connie by surprise.

'Uh okay. It's been so good to meet you. Do you fancy popping around again sometime to help me shift this furniture? I can't think why the room is arranged to face away from the window!'

'A person after my own heart.' Daisy grinned. 'You're on. I'll see you soon – let's face it. Neither of us is going anywhere very far, are we?'

After Daisy had left, Connie hugged her dressing gown close. She wondered how she was going to cope in this strange, beautiful, but brutal world.

# Chapter Five

U nsure of when the working day might begin in this world of permanent daylight, Connie set her portable alarm for 7 a.m., allowing plenty of time for coffee, breakfast and getting dressed. She had only been here a day or two and was already hating the 'toast' which had been provided along with other basic necessities. She made a note to ask Elizabeth how to make the wonderful bread she'd had a few nights ago.

Connie had just finished putting on her parka and the thick, crepe-soaked, waterproof boots that tied up well above the ankle that she had found tucked away beside the freezer, and which, after some deliberation she had decided to wear – as this was to be a boat trip, when Ilannaq appeared.

'Are you ready for a kayak trip and the Inuit?' she asked, archly.

'Too right, I am!' Connie replied with genuine enthusiasm.

'Okay, we go to the Nurse's Station and collect the vaccines and tests, and then go to our kayak down by the jetty.'

Once they had loaded what Connie still thought of as a canoe with the day's supply, Ilannaq explained how to operate the outboard engine, reminding Connie that this was an essential skill in this, sometimes watery, wilderness.

They set off across the bay, and Connie felt a sense of exhilaration like never before. Here was Nurse Sanders flying across the Arctic water – a far cry from the sluice where she had been banished, day after day, by Sister Brown back in Manchester. Once more, she imagined her adventurer grandfather looking on approvingly.

After around ten minutes, a small group of dwellings appeared on the horizon, silhouetted against the bright blue sky. As they drew nearer, the brown smudges materialised into a series of huts and shacks centred around a circular area at the far end of a small jetty.

They arrived, unpacked the canoe and headed for the largest building. 'This is where my father, Moosasee, lives. He is the elder here. If you are offered any food or drink, you must take it, otherwise my people will be insulted. That is one of the first mistakes your predecessor made,' Ilannaq said as they walked.

A tall, well-built man appeared and greeted Ilannaq. '*Ataata*, this is Connie Sanders, the new nurse,' she said.

Moosasee gave Connie a steady, appraising look before shaking hands. '*Atelihai*, Nurse Sanders.' To which she gave a nod, uncertain how to reply.

A further conversation took place in Inuktitut, and Moosasee gestured to a hut on the far side of the settlement.

'We start over there,' said Ilannaq.

They each shouldered a bag and headed for Connie's first patient.

After the glare of the sun and snow, Connie could see nothing inside the dwelling for a few minutes, but once her eyes had adjusted, she once again realised that her expectations had been totally naïve.

Two Inuit sat around a central fire, and as Connie drew closer she could see that they were an elderly man and woman. Ilannaq rattled off a long speech in Inuktitut at which the elderly Inuit nodded and stared at Connie.

'They trust me because I am the elder's daughter. They are happy to have the vaccine, but first they must make you a cup of tea.'

The woman, got to her feet, and with a flourish, produced a battered china teacup from a shelf behind her. She spat in the cup and polished it with a grimy cloth, beaming at Connie. Reaching for a kettle suspended over the fire, she proceeded to pour a cup of very black tea.

Was this where the 'sense of adventure' bit really kicked in? Connie steeled herself not to flinch, putting all thoughts of how TB could be contracted out of her mind. She was going to make a success of this, whatever it took.

Connie dutifully drank while the Inuit couple looked on approvingly.

'Well done. They like you now,' said Ilannaq.

Following the tea ritual, Connie was able to administer vaccines to those who had shown a positive reaction to the tests carried out by her predecessor, without further ado. She also did some basic health checks using her stethoscope and blood pressure kit.

It took most of the day to visit all the dwellings, and to Connie's relief, the tea ceremony was not repeated. Most of the community appeared to be in good health, although one elderly man seemed to have a chest infection. She picked up on his reluctance to be examined and Ilannaq explained that many were frightened of being sent to hospital in Frobisher Bay and never coming back. Connie reassured him that she could give him medicine which she hoped would make him better and made a note to revisit with some antibiotics. Determined not to use any of the 'honey buckets' available – in full view of all and sundry – Connie was grateful to Ilannaq for suggesting a short break halfway through the day, where they returned to her father's dwelling which boasted the luxury of a bucket behind a curtain.

When she eventually got home, and, having divested herself of all the layers, Connie brewed some coffee, opened a tin of soup, and reflected on the day. Her mind was racing to process all the new experiences and sensations. A sense of alarm was still ringing in the back of her mind that she was the only medic for miles – that eventually she would have to do more than simply administer tests and give injections and she hoped she would be able to make contact with Patty and Linda soon. She was thoughtful about the fear and distrust of any Inuit at being sent away from the community and was horrified at stories Ilannaq had told her on their return journey, including references to Inuit children who had been taken away and never returned. Connie, shocked, had asked how long this had been happening, but Ilannaq had remained tight-lipped, obviously not prepared to offer any more information. Connie resolved to ask Daisy whether this was true, and to find out what was going on.

Over the following week Connie and Ilannaq visited several more settlements. Word seemed to have spread and they were generally welcomed, albeit with reluctance in some cases Connie felt, although Ilannaq was quick to assure her that everyone would make her welcome. Connie made a point of eating or drinking anything that was put in front of her, trying not to overthink what she was consuming.

The most challenging of offerings came when they went to visit a settlement celebrating a successful hunting trip. Ilannaq had reminded Connie about eating whatever was offered and that, as this was a special feast, and as she was the guest of honour, she would have first choice of what was on offer. Connie, thinking that food would have been laid out and she could at least choose something that looked vaguely appetising, was horrified when they arrived to find the assembled company sitting in a circle on the floor around a large, central pot, the contents of which were not on view. Once they were seated, Connie, panicking, met Ilannaq's gaze from the other side of the room, from where she had simply nodded and smiled, giving her a thumbs-up.

Connie felt her stomach contract at the thought of what the 'treat' might be, but before she could pursue that thought, she found herself directed to the pot, where the elder and his wife delved in with their hands, indicating for her to follow suit. Heart in her mouth, Connie felt around trying to avoid anything bony, and as her fingers closed on something softer she grew it out of the water and found an eye staring back at her.

Spontaneous applause erupted. 'You have found the tastiest thing of all.' The elder grinned. The ancestors must be pleased. Connie couldn't stop looking at the eye – was it the eye of a fish? – staring back at her, unblinking, and felt bile rise into her throat. But something deep inside triggered an image of her explorer grandfather. Would he have baulked at such a challenge? In her fantasy, she thought not, so closing her eyes, she took a deep breath, willed her stomach to behave, and ate the eye. She imagined being somewhere else - in another time, sitting with her family around the Christmas tree at home, eating Turkish Delight - and chewed firmly, swallowing rapidly. For a split second it was touch and go whether her stomach would accept such a morsel, but in the end mind over matter won the day, and she was able to nod her appreciation, much to the joy of the assembled company.

On their return trip, Ilannaq explained that eyes were a delicacy that the Inuit often saved for their children, believing that they would give them good sight. Connie couldn't help feeling a little smug at this small victory and revelled in Ilannnaq's congratulations, obviously impressed at Connie's strong stomach.

It was a surprise to learn over the first few days that although Ilannaq could speak good English, she was unable to read or write it fluently. She was not embarrassed at this and simply related this fact to Connie with the same equanimity, with which she seemed to view life in general. 'I wasn't good with that at school, so they didn't bother with me. I just made sure I could speak excellent English instead. That seemed more important,' she said, sticking her chest out with pride, and patting herself on the back. 'Am I right?'

'Absolutely right,' Connie concurred. 'I would much rather have your expert memory, and with that there is no need for you to write things down.'

And so, combining their skills, together they created a comprehensive record-keeping system, which Connie updated with great satisfaction, and Ilannaq's approval, at the end of each day.

# Chapter Six

The 2-way radio conversation with the Frobisher Bay doctor had been difficult, as Connie had struggled to manage the technology while writing down the ever-growing list of items he felt she would need if she was going to be able to provide any meaningful healthcare. 'Good luck with getting all that, though, I don't think your predecessor ever got as far as ordering supplies,' had been his final comment.

Connie replaced the radio and updated the list she'd already made – wondering how she would even use some of the things Frobisher Bay had suggested. Sudden footsteps made her jump, and before Connie could gather her thoughts, Paul Archer had materialised in front of her.

'I hear you want to order some supplies.' The patronising tone was unmistakeable.

'Yes, I do.' Connie stood and raised her chin in defiance – just as she had at school when being put down by one of the teachers. 'We don't have even the basics for a functioning medical centre here. I've just been talking to Frobisher Bay, and they've made suggestions which I've added to the list I already made.'

'Right.' Holding out his hand as he stood, Paul said 'Give me the list and I'll see what we can do.'

'Is that it?' Connie had imagined that they would go through the list together, as she knew that the Hudson Bay also had some basic medical provision for their own staff. Naïvely she'd assumed they would be able to work together and share resources.

'I've said, I'll look at it. Now if you don't mind, I've things to do.'

Connie stared at the space where Paul had stood, stunned for a few moments. And then an all-consuming panic set in – because this wasn't school, this was the real world where people's lives were at stake.

What was she doing here? How did she think she, Connie Sanders, could even begin to deal with the challenges of this place, this job, and the likes of Paul Archer? She felt like a child who had just given in her homework and could already feel the familiar toxic mixture of anger and fear brewing. The heady sense of being grown-up and capable had disappeared almost as soon as it arrived – a fleeting sensation. She sat, motionless, in front of the radio, frozen in time and unable to move for what seemed like hours. Fortunately, no one came into the office. A shouting match between two of the Hudson Bay men, outside, brought Connie back to reality, and looking at the clock on the wall she could see that only five minutes had passed. Gripping the edge of the desk with both hands, she took a deep breath, thought once more of the courage of the Arctic explorers of the past, and willed herself to get up and walk home. At least she wasn't lost and stranded in a white wilderness as they had been, although at times like today, it had felt a bit like it.

Determined to put the episode with Paul behind her, Connie had taken up Elizabeth's offer to teach her how to make bread, Arctic style, and now they were putting Connie's kitchen to good use. Having mixed the flour, water and dried yeast, they were both kneading the dough in companionable silence. Connie felt her movements falling into a rhythm as she folded, turned and kneaded. The process was strangely calming and homely.

Once the dough had been left to rise, they sat with cups of coffee, Connie feeling the effects of a good work-out and rubbing her aching arms. Elizabeth laughed. 'You'll soon get muscles like this.' She flexed her arm. Connie somehow doubted that her body would ever produce an athletic physique to match Elizabeth's

'Thank you so much, Elizabeth, for helping me with this, and letting me have the yeast.' A search of the cupboards in Connie's kitchen had revealed several bags of flour, but no yeast. 'Your predecessor was no cook,' Elizabeth had commented before returning home to get some yeast, bringing back enough for Connie to bake several more loaves. 'You'll be able to get some from the Bay shop. If they run out, everyone has to wait for the sea-lift to come. It shouldn't be long, now that break-up is well under way.'

After a couple of sips, Elizabeth continued, 'You know, when I first came to the Arctic, someone taught me how to make bread like this and it was a life-saver, so I'm just passing on the knowledge – Arctic mother to Arctic daughter.' She smiled, before adding, 'Not that I'm anywhere near old enough to be your mother though!'

As they surveyed the landscape, Elizabeth turned to Connie. 'Seriously though, how old *are* you?'

For a moment, Connie considered lying about her age to seem more grown-up than she really was but quickly dismissed the idea. Did she really want to go down that road – starting with lies?

'I'm twenty-one,' she answered.

At Elizabeth's intake of breath, Connie turned. 'What?'

'You must be either mad or brave. Or a bit of both, like me. I was nineteen when I first came over here from Scotland. I was madly in love and would have followed Peter anywhere. Still would,' she added. 'But at least I wasn't on my own.'

'If I'm honest, I'm probably a bit of both, too. But I like to think I'm more brave than stupid,' Connie added, sensing the young-adult defensiveness in her tone and wishing she had kept her mouth shut. Would she never learn to think before she spoke, opening herself up to people far too easily, being far too trusting? Her mother had been right when she'd said Connie had 'MUG' written on her forehead. Look what she'd let Helen do to her.

Elizabeth gave her a gentle look, as if sensing these confusing thoughts going though Connie's mind.

'How do your family feel about you coming so far from home?'

Connie pondered the question before answering, warning herself not to reveal more than necessary. 'I don't think they're that happy about it, but they didn't say much, so I guess it's okay.'

'But it's the first time you've lived away from home...from Manchester?'

'Yes, apart from the Nurse's Home, but I still went home on my days off – my mum seemed to expect it.'

'Well, if it helps, I agree with you. You are definitely more brave than foolish. Something tells me you're made of stern stuff to have even made it this far.' Elizabeth stood. 'Let's see if that bread's ready for another round of kneading.'

Knocking back the dough and going through the kneading process again was becoming hard going and Connie found herself taking constant breaks, rubbing her sore arms.

'You have to keep going, Connie. Think of someone that you would really like to give a pummelling to. I'll bet there's someone.' Elizabeth said without breaking her rhythm.

Despite her best efforts, the inevitable vision of Helen appeared, and Connie found that she had much more energy in reserve than she realised.

Once the loaves were baking in the oven, and as a wonderful smell of home filled her house, Connie thought of her mother, making bread like this, two or three times a week. She and her brother had no idea of the work that had gone into the toast and sandwiches they had consumed without thought.

'I'm wondering who you were thinking of? You were certainly giving that dough some. Who gave you so much energy...and anger?'

Elizabeth was never less than forthright, Connie was learning. But Helen was back in her box now, thoroughly pummelled and with the lid fastened shut.

'Oh just one of the sisters on the ward,' she answered untruthfully.

She was grateful that Elizabeth didn't comment or ask any further questions.

# Chapter Seven

C onnie had been too busy with work and baking bread to think much more about rearranging her furniture, but even so, was glad when the whirlwind that was Daisy burst through her door one evening.

'I haven't forgotten your request for my furniture moving services, so here I am, all yours. My only fee is a cup of coffee...and is that something wonderful I can smell baking?'

'Indeed it is. The wonderful Elizabeth has shown me how to make bread, so you're just in time. Next on the list is learning how to make ice cream.'

'Oh wow! I can see I'm going to be spending a lot of time here.'

Connie smiled and felt a thrill that this woman wanted to spend time with her – even though the promise of fresh bread and ice cream might well have been a factor.

Once they had rearranged the surprisingly heavy furniture, they were glad to sit down with coffee and slices of fresh bread, loaded with jam, and admire the view across the bay.

'How could anyone sit with their back to this?' Connie gestured, sweeping her arm across the vista before them.

'I think your predecessor maybe didn't want any reminder of where she was. From what I hear, she couldn't get back to Australia fast enough, poor thing.'

They munched in companionable silence for a few minutes.

'What about you, Nurse Sanders? How are you feeling a few weeks in? Are you about to leave us all and scoot off back to Manchester?'

'The short answer is, no, but I can't pretend that life Harbour-Inlet style isn't taking a bit of getting used to.' Connie paused and took a sip of coffee, before answering with determined conviction. 'But I don't feel like turning my back on it, just yet.'

'What about the home counties household?' Daisy grinned mischievously. 'Have you been given the once over by Ma Brooks yet?'

'I have, and I think I deflected most questions pretty well, and convinced her that I didn't have a boyfriend to run home to.'

Daisy studied her for a moment. 'Oh God, that one! I think I'm exempt as I'm married – in name only though. And that's going to change as soon as I can make it happen.'

'Oh!' Somehow Connie hadn't even considered that Daisy might be married.

Daisy threw back her head and let out a great laugh. 'I know! But it was a huge mistake and I'm not really wife material. I just wanted to get married and get it over with, I think. To stop my mother going on about my spinster status. So I married Ralph, who I met at one of her 'tea parties' and who turned out to be an utter bastard, controlling and...violent.'

Connie couldn't stop the gasp that escaped her lips. 'Oh Daisy, I'm so sorry.'

'Yes, well, it's in the past now. And I'll certainly be avoiding anything like that happening again. I have no wish to be beaten black and blue just because I don't have a meal ready on time.' Daisy pressed her lips together. 'Can you believe that my mother tried to make me stay with him, even when I told her what was happening?'

Connie took the question to be rhetorical and could think of nothing useful to say anyway, so stayed silent.

'So I upped sticks, took as much of his money as I could and ended up here.' There was a forced humour in her tone that smacked of a well-buried anger. Connie recognised it all too well, and said nothing.

Daisy stood up and took the cups. 'Sorry. I don't know where that came from. Anyway, it's ancient history, or will be soon, I hope. Want a refill?' She spoke with her back to Connie, turning abruptly, as if physically changing the subject.

'By the way, I've spoken with Patty and she can radio you tomorrow afternoon at around 2 o'clock, if you can be there.'

'I will. Thanks Daisy.' Connie felt a thrill of excitement at having a colleague, no matter how inaccessible.

'So, tell me about the Inuit you've visited. How have things been?'

Connie soon had Daisy in tears of laughter as she related tales of teacups and honey buckets, finishing with the eye challenge.

'But seriously though, it sounds like you've gained some respect. The Inuit are a proud people and they don't take well to being patronised. We're lucky to have Ilannaq. She is so much more than just an interpreter – she is a bridge between our world and theirs. Follow her advice and you won't go too wrong. But as regards delicious Inuit fare, it can be a mixed experience.'

Connie sat forward and rested her arms on her knees, clasping her hands. Serious now, weighing up how to approach the subject that was worrying away at the back of her mind. She took a breath and plunged in. 'I've noticed that some Inuit are reluctant to admit to any illness because they fear going to Frobisher Bay. There are stories about adults – and children never coming back. I'm not surprised they don't trust us if this is true. Do you know anything about this? Surely their fears are unfounded.'

Daisy turned her gaze to the sparkling blue water in the bay before answering. 'Yes the rumours are true.'

Connie couldn't stifle a gasp of horror. 'What?'

'The Canadian government has had a policy for some time of wiping out Inuit culture and Westernising them as a people. They take the children and educate them in special schools in Canada where speaking in Inuktitut is forbidden, as is anything relating to their culture. They are taught to be Christians. And sometimes older Inuit are not returned to their communities if they're not well enough.'

Connie felt as if she was drifting into the realms of nightmare. Surely this couldn't be true. No one had told her about this!

'You know this, how?'

'Because I've visited the schools. I do work for the Canadian government, remember.'

Connie stood up and moved away. 'So you're part of this...this terrible thing? But I thought you hated the way the Inuit culture was disappearing.'

'Yes I do. I'm an anthropologist so of course I'm interested in studying cultures and communities. And yes, I am passionate about not letting Westernisation destroy the life of the Inuit. So the studies I carry out mean I can report back to the Canadian government aspects of Inuit culture that are important to retain, and make an argument as to why. I can't single-handedly change government policy, but I figure I can do more from the inside, from a position of influence than I can by holding a placard in a demonstration in Ottawa.'

'But I thought you were on their side! What was all that about the dog teams you were telling me? Now you're saying you're part of what's happening?' Connie felt her cheeks flushing in anger.

After a silence, Daisy said, 'Don't be too quick to judge, Connie, nothing in this world is ideal. But we, you and I, have some influence to do our bit, so it's important to use it carefully.' There was an edge to her voice.

'But what if I need to send someone to hospital? I can't do that knowing they might never return.'

'Like I said, there is no place for idealism in this place. If you have to send someone to hospital you will hopefully be saving their life, which, at the end of the day, is why you're here.'

'I'm not here to separate patients from their families to be indoctrinated into a culture that's not theirs, however you try to sugar-coat it.' Connie could feel herself quivering with rage – and yes there was disappointment in there somewhere – disappointment that Daisy wasn't who she had seemed. Someone who could callously marry a man knowing she didn't love him. Someone who could stand by and see a people humiliated.

As the silence lengthened, Daisy got up abruptly and headed for the door. Connie didn't move. As she was putting her boots on Daisy threw a barb over her shoulder that struck Connie right in the middle of her chest. 'Grow up, Connie! This place is not for faint-hearted romantics!' And with that, she was gone.

Connie knew she would have to think about this unexpected ethical dilemma, and felt deeply uncomfortable that she hadn't been adequately prepared for the realities of this job. 'A sense of adventure' had not been an accurate job description on any level – she wasn't on an Enid Blyton adventure – no matter how the Brooks's tried to recreate that environment in their home. One thing she determined though, and that was she was going to learn as much as possible and get as much equipment as she could to avoid sending any of the Inuit to hospital. On an intellectual level she understood what Daisy had meant. But the way in which the rebuke – because that's what it was – was delivered had been harsh and uncalled-for. Connie was relieved in a strange way that there was something to dislike about Daisy. Even so, she felt hot self-pitying tears on her cheeks as all the energy and drive she had summoned up dissipated in the empty house.

# Chapter Eight

The radio conversation with Patty lifted Connie's spirits, and once she had once again got used to the mechanics of using the system, remembering to say 'Roger', and, 'over', pressing a button when it was Patty's turn to speak, the conversation flowed easily.

'How are you doing about getting supplies and equipment? I hear Paul Archer is not the easiest man to deal with.'

Connie glanced, furtively over her shoulder before answering. 'Not easy. I don't even know if he will order the things I've asked for. Things Frobisher Bay suggested.'

'Well, I'd wait and see what you get, and then let me know. I'll go through the list with you and tell you which things I think are essential. Then you can insist on those. I think it's best to choose your battles with him.'

Connie smiled at the Irish accent.

'And I hear that you've met our Daisy.'

'Yes.' Connie deliberated whether to say more and chose not to mention the way their last meeting had ended.

Possibly sensing some tension in her answer, Patty replied. 'She's definitely taken a liking to you, and Daisy doesn't suffer fools lightly.'

'Well, I think after our last conversation, I'm definitely in the "fool" category.'

Connie was relieved that Patty didn't ask for details. 'Don't worry, she'll soon get over it.'

Connie didn't know whether *she* would, though.

A few days later, on her now familiar walk to the Nurse's Station, Connie came across Esther talking animatedly in rapid Inuktitut with some Inuit girls. They appeared to be playing with a group of small children. She gave Connie a shy wave and smiled.

'I'm helping look after the children,' she volunteered.

'It looks fun. What are you playing?'

'I'm trying to teach them What's the Time Mr Wolf? I used to play it with my friends at school when I was little,' Esther added, seeming to feel that some explanation was needed. 'I love playing with the little ones, and I'm hoping to help out a bit in school next term.'

'Good for you, Esther! Do you miss your old school? Was it in England?'

'It was a long time ago and my mum and dad teach me now.'

Connie felt the girl's shyness and tried another tack to engage her in conversation. 'So what's your favourite subject?'

'I'm quite good at maths which my mum used to teach back in England, and my dad is teaching me Latin and French.'

'Poor you, I hated French at school and was never good enough to get into the Latin set.' The words were out before Connie could stop them, before she realised that she was being insensitive. She hurriedly tried to recover the situation by adding, 'Of course, it's not the same for everybody. I'm sure you're brilliant at it.'

Esther had retreated behind a thick curtain of hair.

Connie tried to revive the flagging conversation. 'So what do you like best?'

Just as the silence had convinced her that the conversation was well and truly over, Esther lifted her head and looked at Connie. 'I love reading and writing stories, but I've read all my books about three times, and it takes ages for the sea-lift to arrive.'

Connie grasped the lifeline. 'Me too, I've always loved reading!' Encouraged by a tentative smile, she continued, 'I've got some books that you could borrow. Why don't you pop round later and visit my library?' Connie made inverted comma signs with her fingers at the word 'library'.

Esther giggled and for the first time Connie saw something of the girl beneath the reserve. 'Really? Could I? That would be wonderful! Thanks Connie.'

Connie returned the smile, relieved to have re-established communication and looked forward to getting to know this girl who was so much like her younger self.

Later, there was a tentative knock. By now, used to Daisy and Elizabeth simply walking in, she hurried to open the door.

'Oh hello, Esther. Come in. I'm so pleased you came!'

Having taken off her boots, Connie was amused to see Esther covertly studying the room. 'I haven't quite got everything sorted yet, and I couldn't bring too much stuff with me,' Connie said as Esther's gaze came to rest on the small bookcase. 'But there is no way I was going anywhere without my favourite books. What sort of things do you like?'

'I don't know, really.' Connie's heart went out in sympathy as Esther blushed.

'Okay, let's have a look. What about *Lorna Doone*? Have you read that? It's very romantic.'

'My mum is quite strict about what I read – I'm not sure if she would want me to read something like that.' Esther shifted uncomfortably on the floor, hiding her face once again behind the curtain of hair.

'Oh, come on, surely a bit of harmless romance isn't a problem.'

Connie was met once more with a wall of silence as Esther refused to meet her eye, and cursed herself for being so insensitive, yet again.

'Okay, so what about *Black Beauty*? Do you like horses?'

'I love animals!' Esther responded eagerly, lifting her head to reveal girlish enthusiasm. She took the book, opening it with a reverence that brought unexpected tears to Connie's eyes. 'Although I haven't seen any horses for a long time, she said tracing the outline of Black Beauty on one of the coloured plates with her finger.'

'Do you miss England?'

'I don't really remember much as I haven't been there since I was six, but I do miss trees, flowers...and dogs...and definitely horses!' She smiled.

Connie took a steadying breath. 'Right-ho! *Black Beauty* it is! Take it and let me know what you think when you've read it.'

'Thanks Connie.' Esther hurried to put her boots on. 'I need to get back – my parents will be wondering where I am,' she threw over her shoulder, already out of the door.

It hadn't occurred to her that Esther might not have told her parents where she was going. Connie mentally shrugged – it was what twelve-year-olds did wasn't it? Sneaking off with their friends?

The next morning, just as Connie was setting out, she saw Mrs Brooks striding in her direction. She stood and waited as the older woman approached at speed, feeling an increasing sense of apprehension.

'Good morning, Mrs Brooks.' Connie was determined to be professional.

'How dare you...' Connie took a step back at the force of the older woman's anger.

'I'm sorry?'

'How dare you try to corrupt my daughter's mind? Luring her to your house behind my back!'

Connie tried not to notice the spittle at the corner of her mouth. 'I'm sorry... I didn't—'

'Just because you're new here, you think you can take liberties. Well let me tell you, it won't happen again. I'll be watching.'

Connie recollected the binoculars and felt a return of the unease she had felt when she'd seen them on the windowsill at the Brooks's. 'I'm so sorry, Mrs Brooks, I honestly didn't mean any harm.'

'Well, we'll say no more for now.' Mrs Brooks strode off as rapidly as she'd approached.

Connie put her hand against the wall and waited several minutes until her heart stopped racing. As she walked to the Nurse's Station a sense of anger started to take root. Anger on Esther's behalf as well as her own. This woman was the incarnation of Sister Potts, the tyrant who'd ruled the men's surgical ward with a rod of iron, back in Manchester, just in another guise, in a different world. Connie reflected that women like this were perhaps to be found wherever you ran to. She worried about the fate of *Black Beauty* and whether she would ever see her precious book again.

# Chapter Nine

The first wave of homesickness caught Connie by surprise. She had not heard or felt its approach until it hit her hard, knocking her to the ground.

The first, awkward and complicated radio conversation with her parents had been made worse by the fact that every time Connie said 'Roger', her mother assumed she was mentioning someone she'd met. Connie hadn't been prepared for the effect the sound of her parents' voices would have, sounding ghostly and distant, thousands of miles away. It seemed that everything familiar, everything that was her world was on a distant planet, out of reach.

'Who is this Roger, Connie?'

'It's no one, Mum. It's just what we say when it's the other person's turn to speak.' Connie's mother digested this in silence. Connie was determined to keep her feelings from showing in her voice, not wanting to worry her mum and dad, not wanting to have failed already. She cast around in her mind for something mundane to say, but came up with nothing.

'Did you get our letters?' Connie was grateful as her father spoke for the first time, breaking the silence.

'Not yet, Dad, we haven't had many flights in because of the weather. I expect they'll all come at once and then I'll have a feast,' said Connie, trying to lighten the mood.

'It's been raining here – typical summer weather. It's probably as cold as where you are.' Connie smiled at the British preoccupation with the weather – a go-to solution to oil the wheels of any difficult conversation. She imagined her father's beloved roses hanging their heads in the damp, British summer and looked out of the window at the crystal waters, and sparkling ice in the glare of the Arctic sunshine and knew that she was in a different world.

'I need to go, someone else is waiting to use the radio.' From the corner of her eye she could see Jim Briggs waiting, and heard his restless fidgeting. 'I love you both, and don't worry about me. Everything's fine.' Connie mustered up the courage to keep control.

She heard a muffled 'Bye Connie.' and was that a 'We love you,' from her father?

Connie could feel her composure crumbling and was desperate to escape from the Hudson Bay office before she fell to pieces in front of Jim. Taking a deep breath, she stood and headed for the door without acknowledging his presence.

'How are things in good old Manchester?' Connie stood with her hand on the door and turned.

'You know Manchester?'

'Salford, born and bred,' he answered, hand on chest and giving a little bow.

'Old Trafford,' Connie ventured. Suddenly the irrational urge to cling onto the life raft of shared experience with this strange little man with wondering hands was overwhelming. 'Just as always – lots of rain.' She grinned through the pain.

'We'll have to catch up and talk more Manchester, sometime, get a break from all these Canadians. I've got to get on the radio now though, sorry.' He fluttered his butterfly hands in the direction of the radio.

'Okay, yes...of course.'

She saw Paul Archer approaching behind Jim. *Please no. not now*. He strode up and waved her list in front of her face. Jim made a hasty exit, muttering about making his phone call.

Her legs shaking, Connie sat back down in the chair she had just vacated. 'You're not running a hospital here, this is a small nurse's station in a remote settlement. You shouldn't let those Frobisher Bay doctors talk you into ridiculous demands,' he sneered and took a step back. 'Do you even know what all these things are and how to use them?'

'Well, I—'

'I thought not. I've ordered what I think you'll need and the rest you can forget about.' He thrust the paper into her lap before striding away.

Connie hurled herself out into the glare of the sun and ran as fast as her footwear and cumbersome clothing would allow, back to the security of her new home. Closing the door and leaning against its reassuring bulk, her breath came in short gasps. It was a few minutes before she had the strength to divest herself of her coat and boots and, with shaking hands, put a pot of coffee on along with some toast. As the reassuring scents wafted through her home, Connie sat on her bed in the yellow dressing gown, retreating to an inner sanctuary.

Now that she had made the toast, she couldn't bring herself to eat it, and only took a few bites. She fortified herself with the coffee, now laced with a generous shot of whisky. And huddling under the comfort of the blankets, Connie felt her breath slowing and a warmth returning to her body. Her hands had at last ceased shaking as she wrapped them around the warm mug. Her mind was numb and her thoughts unfocused as she shut down, distancing herself from the fearful world outside the door, even outside the nest she had made as she curled in her bed.

# Chapter Ten

W hen she came to, lying under the covers of her bed, memories of the humiliation she had felt at the hands of Paul Archer, and of the attacking anger of Mrs Brooks, were almost too much to bear. She closed her eyes and balled her fists, willing them both to disappear. Connie thought about her old life – the life she had fled; her friends – fellow nurses who she had abruptly left behind without any thought or explanation in her race to get away; her bewildered parents; the trees, flowers and countryside she had taken for granted on her childhood cycle rides with her father and David – he lagging behind, hating every outdoor moment. The bustle and constant movement of a large city. Parties and dancing with some of the other nurses, and her beloved cinema. Connie had abandoned all that to come to this wasteland, where she had been humiliated and bullied all over again. The realisation that this place was no different from the world she had left behind, except it had snow...and fewer people, made the hurt even more potent. That in such a small group of people, everything, the humiliation and bullying she was running from was present in this remote place, and with a more powerful, undiluted force. She closed her eyes, willing the darkness of sleep to return and take all the pain away. She would go home

– running had got her nowhere. Her thoughts drifted back to what she was running from. Where had it all started?

The TV in the student nurses' common room had broken down. The 'lower orders' were strictly prohibited from entering the trained staff quarters which housed the other television, but Connie and some of her partners in crime had gone to the senior common room anyway. The room was full of red-belts – third-year nurses, but, ever the rebel, Connie had walked boldly forward and sat on the sofa right in front of the TV. Laurence Olivier was doing his stuff in a film version of *Pride and Prejudice*, and Connie had always been a sucker for romance. The nurse beside her, smiled and said she could be forgiven if she could hold on to Connie while Olivier was on, as he was her absolute idol. Connie, remembering her mother's warnings, and had stiffened, resisting the temptation to enjoy physical contact with this girl who expressed herself so freely and unselfconsciously. But then she turned and looked at Helen, and that was that.

As their friendship blossomed, with her mother's warnings banished from her mind, Connie had bloomed in the sunshine of the romantic poetry they'd shared and the bliss of Rachmaninov and Chopin that Helen had introduced her to. Even though she didn't really understand what she was feeling, she'd been swept away by it, imagining them being friends...or something...for ever. And then, just as suddenly, it was over as Helen announced she was getting married and handed in her notice.

Connie had floundered in the morass of her confused thinking. Getting married was what people did wasn't it? So what was the matter with her? Why hadn't Helen talked about it? Shared it with her? What did she think she and Helen had, anyway? However she tried to rationalise what had happened, over the following weeks, there was no escaping the devastation, humiliation and despair Connie had felt – and still did, when she allowed herself to think about it. And now, here was Daisy, who had done exactly the same thing, who had got married because it was expected, and somewhere, deep down, Connie knew that had been the reason for Helen's hasty marriage. The only good thing was that she hadn't allowed Daisy to get to her before finding out about the truth, because she knew the potential was there for her to have similar feelings for Daisy, even if she didn't understand them. She took comfort in the fact that Daisy was as different as Helen as chalk and cheese. A small smile appeared as she imagined Daisy being forced to read romantic poetry or listen to Chopin. No, she was no Helen, but Connie would be careful all the same – Daisy had the potential to do the same as Helen – after all, she'd already done it once, hadn't she?

Where could she go from here? There seemed to be no future for her. If she couldn't escape humiliation at the ends of the earth, where was there to go? Home, where at least there was a familiar world. As soon as she felt stronger Connie resolved she would make arrangements to go home and accept that she was not an adventurer after all. Having made the decision, eventually the merciful oblivion of sleep returned.

'Connie, Connie, are you alright? Are you ill?' Elizabeth was sitting on the bed, gently caressing Connie's shoulder.

'What...?'

'No one has seen you since yesterday, and we were worried.'

This triggered a bout of sobbing as the pain Connie had escaped in sleep returned with a vengeance. 'Oh sweetheart. What is it?' She could hear concern in Elizabeth's voice.

'I don't want to wake up, leave me alone.' She wrenched her shoulder from under Elizabeth's hand. 'I want to go home. I miss everything at home so much. I don't know what I'm even doing here.' Connie was conscious of the unattractive whining and snivelling noises that felt as if they were being physically wrenched from her heart. 'I've decided to go home. Everything's gone wrong. Paul Archer thinks I'm useless. Mrs Brooks hates me...and...and I can't do this. I'll radio Frobisher Bay to get me out of here.'

'You're homesick,' said Elizabeth, soothing. 'Come here, you poor thing.' She held and rocked Connie who, when spent, eventually became still in her arms.

Connie felt the warmth of Elizabeth's body through her sweater, and strong arms around her. She felt safer than she had felt for a very long time.

As if sensing this, eventually Elizabeth put her hands on Connie's shoulders and drew her away, lifting her chin with one hand. 'This was bound to happen – you are so young, and you've taken on a huge challenge. Not just in coming here, but in dealing with whatever drove you here in the first place. Because I know there was something.' She gave Connie a searching look. Elizabeth took Connie's hand. 'Whenever this happens, and it will from time to time, come and find me, and if I'm not here, find something to occupy your mind – I would suggest gardening, but that's not going to happen here.' Connie managed a wry smile. 'But do some baking, read a book, write a journal. Maybe take up photography – Peter could send you a camera. I noticed how interested you were. But most of all, don't be hard on yourself – this was never going to be easy, and you'll never forgive yourself if you give up now. You've already got further than your predecessor.'

Connie looked out across the bay. 'I can't do it. I'm a failure and I need to go home.' Her voice seemed strangely detached from her body.

'But you already *are* doing it!'

As Connie put her head in her hands, Elizabeth continued in a low, firm voice, 'I said I sensed a steeliness in you, and I still do. I know you can do this. Don't think too far ahead, just take the next step.'

Connie didn't move.

'And remember, you have friends who will support you, and who are on your side. You have me, Ilannaq, and Daisy too, if you'll let her in.'

'But you'll be gone in a few months.' Connie could hear the unattractive whine in her voice.

'Don't think about that. Think about today. And I am with you today, and tomorrow, and the day after that. That's all you need to think about for now.'

Connie lifted her head.

'There, you've taken the first step. Look at me.'

Connie looked deep into Elizabeth's eyes and somehow felt some of the strength they contained filter through into her own mind. Maybe she could take another step.

'Come on, a cup of tea and some of my best bread are in order, I think. Do you think you could get dressed and wash those tears off that lovely face while I do that?'

Connie caught her breath. No one had ever described her face as lovely, never mind any other attribute. Eventually she nodded, and while she washed her face, she could hear the comforting sound of Elizabeth bustling about in the kitchen.

When they were seated facing the ocean, Connie, revived by the coffee and toast, turned to Elizabeth. 'Thank you so much, Elizabeth. What would I do without you?' She could feel the tears prickling in her eyes again.

'Actually, I was also looking for you to tell you that we've had a delivery and some of the medical supplies you ordered have arrived.'

Connie felt an alertness returning. 'The supplies? They can't have, I only spoke to Paul yesterday.'

'Well there are definitely some boxes labelled Nurse's Station, as well as some letters addressed to you – but maybe save those when you're feeling stronger,' Elizabeth added.

'How did I miss that?'

'Well, you've been holed up for at least twenty-four hours and the flight came at short notice. Didn't you hear the phone?'

Connie glanced at the phone on the table. 'One ring for the RMCP,' she murmured, remembering the instructions from Rev Brooks on the day of her arrival. He had written the code for the phone system next to the strange instrument that looked half phone and half wind-up radio. She knew the code for medical help was two rings, but fortunately she had not experienced that so far.

'Right...okay... I need to get myself together.' Connie sat up and pushed her short hair back from her face with both hands, tucking it behind her ears.

Elizabeth smiled. 'That's my girl! Go get 'em. But sustenance first.' She sternly pointed at the remaining toast.

Opening the boxes and examining the contents, Connie saw that many of the basics she had ordered had arrived. She sat back, thinking. There was only one explanation – Paul had ordered these items as soon as she'd given him the list, but had chosen to wait nearly a week before telling her. Another small way of undermining any fragile authority she might have. Panic and anger hovering, she remembered what Elizabeth had said – one day at a time. This was an issue for another day. In the meantime, she at least had most of the basics she would need for a functioning Nurse's Station.

After several hours of itemising and sorting the delivery, Connie felt that the room was beginning to look something like a medical facility. She had gone through everything with Ilannaq, trying to learn some of the Inuktitut names for various items. The letters on thin blue airmail paper, she put to one side taking Elizabeth's advice to leave them until she was feeling stronger. It would most likely be some time before any others arrived, so there was no rush. Instead, she spent the next few evenings revisiting old friends on her bookshelf, losing herself in the world of Elizabeth Bennet and Jane Austen's Bath, followed by Thomas Hardy and the ill-fated Tess, in another time and place.

It was just as Tess was working away in Farmer Groby's potato field, late one afternoon, that the phone rang twice. Connie froze, waiting for a third ring, the signal for Rev Brooks, which never came.

Reluctantly, she picked up the heavy receiver. 'Hello?'

'Connie?' Ilannaq's voice rang out into the room.

'What is it?'

'Can you come? Moosa is in agony with a toothache. We're at the Nurse's Station.'

Before she could overthink anything, Connie threw on several layers and rushed along the well-trodden path to the station. Ilannaq was waiting for her in the doorway and indicated Moosa sitting on the floor, his head in his hands.

'Okay, let's take a look.' Connie crouched beside him. 'Tell him that I'm not going to hurt him, I'm just taking a look,' she said over her shoulder.

It soon became apparent that Moosa could hardly speak. She turned his swollen face towards her and signalled for him to open his mouth which he did reluctantly. The gum was swollen, and infection had already set in, the tooth would have to come out. Connie stood up and sorted out some painkillers and antibiotics, all the while telling Ilannaq what she was doing. After much persuasion, Moosa swallowed the pills and Ilannaq took him home.

Connie spent the rest of the evening looking through the medical books she had brought, frantically searching for anything on tooth extractions. After a sleepless night, she rang the doctor in Frobisher Bay, who arranged for a dentist to call her back. He, in turn, gave her instructions as to where to inject the anaesthetic (which fortunately had been included in the unexpected delivery) and how to remove the tooth. As she returned to the Nurse's Station the following day, Connie rehearsed the procedure over and over in her head.

She and Ilannaq conferred about how to best tackle the extraction, and once the necessary anaesthetic had been prepared and the needle prepped, Ilannaq set off to find Moosa and bring him to the surgery. He eventually appeared with much reluctance, having said to Ilannaq that he felt much better now and didn't need to see Nurse Sanders. Ilannaq had managed to persuade him that this was the effect of the painkillers, and that the actual problem hadn't gone away. He sat on the bed, his hands clenched in his lap, as Connie put on surgical gloves and picked up the syringe. Taking a deep breath she turned, hiding the needle behind her, and signalled to him to open his mouth. As she drew near she saw the fear in Moosa's eyes turn to terror as he saw the needle coming towards him in less than steady hands.

He was gone before Connie could curse herself for not telling him to close his eyes. However, having watched him rapidly recede into the distance, Connie and Ilannaq shared a look that contained more than a little relief.

News spread rapidly of Moosa's miraculous cure with Nurse Sanders' magic tablets and no mention was made of the needle. When Connie came across Moosa a few days later, proudly sporting a gap between his teeth, she decided not to ask any questions.

Even though her patient had fled in terror before she could carry out the procedure, the fact that Connie had switched into nurse mode and had not panicked, and that people were realising that Nurse Sanders could make a difference made her feel stronger somehow, even if there was talk of magic pills, which created an uneasiness in Connie about the fact that she hadn't actually treated Moosa. The last thing she wanted was for the Inuit to become reliant on medication that masked the real problem. But for now, she remembered her resolve to be able to treat as many Inuit as possible within Harbour Inlet. She might be naïve and idealistic, but she was determined to do as much as she could, and so, the next day, she harnessed her anger at the injustice of the Canadians and steeled herself to face Paul, rehearsing carefully what she was going to say. Following another conversation with Patty, she now had a list of things that she was prepared to fight for.

This time, not allowing him to catch her unawares, she remained standing and looked him in the eye. 'I need some of the other items on the list if I'm going to do my job properly, and if you're not going to order them for me, I'm going to contact the government offices in Montreal, direct. I know what I'm doing, but I can't help people if I don't have the right equipment.' Connie inwardly marvelled at the calm authority in her voice. Where had that come from? Suddenly, she felt ten feet tall as she held Paul's gaze.

'You've got some spirit, Nurse Sanders, I'll give you that.' But his eyes were cold. 'Very well, I'll put the order in, and we'll see what happens, shall we?'

As there was nothing further to be said, she finished with, 'Thank you, Paul.'

'Don't be surprised if none of it turns up though.' Connie ignored him as she was already out of the door.

# Chapter Eleven

The next time the phone rang once, Connie was ready for it, and along with everyone else in the settlement picked up the receiver to listen in to the call. The long-awaited annual sea-lift was imminent, and the ship had been sighted. A festive atmosphere broke out as everyone excitedly reminded each other what they had ordered, although Connie, who had arrived too late to place an order would have to wait and see what her predecessor had ordered on her behalf. From what she had heard about Pam, she wasn't holding out much hope.

Within an hour the settlement was gathered at the water's edge, eagerly scanning both the horizon and Mrs Brooks, who, as the owner of the only pair of binoculars was revelling in her brief moment of popularity. Connie found herself next to Peter, busy recording the occasion with his camera. She watched enviously as he committed the event to film which would eventually become prints for people in the future to look back on. Seeing her interest, Peter explained how the camera worked and even allowed her to take some shots, explaining carefully how to create the best results.

From the corner of her eye, Connie noticed Esther hovering on the edge of the crowd and took advantage of Mrs Brooks and her binoculars being otherwise occupied to ask about *Black Beauty*.

Glancing at her mother's back, Esther turned to Connie. 'I loved it! I felt as if I was really there. I'm so glad it had a happy ending.' She spoke, rushing to get the words out.

'Okay, what about another one? Or are you getting some books on the sea-lift?'

'I heard about my mother being angry with you,' she said, ignoring the question. 'I'm sorry.' The curtain of hair fell forward again as Esther looked at the ground moving her foot from side to side.

'You shouldn't be sorry, you haven't done anything wrong, but next time I'll ask her before you come round. How would that be?'

Esther nodded. 'I think she was mostly angry because she didn't know I was coming. She hates it when she doesn't know things. I asked my father if I could have some more pens and special books to write in. I want to write my own stories.' Esther returned to the original question. 'And maybe some new books.' She lifted her head and there was a hint of a smile.

Connie turned and looked into Esther's hazel eyes. 'When you get your first book published, be sure to autograph one for me. You'll have stories to tell that no other English girl will have experienced.'

Esther lifted her head, slicked her hair behind her ears and looked steadily into Connie's eyes. 'You're serious, aren't you?'

'Absolutely. Why shouldn't I be? Any time you want to borrow more books, let me know and I'll check with your mother. Keep *Black Beauty* – as a present from me.' Much as Connie treasured the book, it somehow felt the right thing to do.

While they'd been talking, the ship had appeared and could be seen as a speck on the horizon with the naked eye. A cheer went up at the sight of this nautical Father Christmas, and everyone waited impatiently as the speck grew larger. Eventually, several smaller boats, sprightly offspring of the mother ship, could be seen heading their way. As the first crunched its way onto the foreshore, a spontaneous cheer and round of applause erupted from the assembled company.

The RMCP chief and Paul Archer set up a makeshift distribution hub on the shore, and Connie was amazed at the efficiency with which all the crates and boxes were either distributed on the spot, loaded onto the backs of makeshift sleds, or taken by the large, tracked Hudson Bay vehicle to be stored in their warehouse, awaiting collection or delivery by Innik. Even though most of the goodies couldn't be accessed immediately, it still seemed important to be present for their arrival, and most stayed to watch the unloading.

Connie became aware of Elizabeth standing beside them, and Esther looked down as Tom tugged on her hand.

'I knew you could do it!' Elizabeth squeezed Connie's arm.

Connie smiled, unused to anyone having confidence in her ability to do anything.

'I ordered more medical supplies as a priority shipping – I hope some of them will come. I've noticed that alcohol seems to come pretty quickly, so I'm hoping medical supplies will be treated as equally important.' Connie could hear the sarcasm in her own voice

'Mmm, I heard about your showdown with Paul. Well done! Keep channelling that warrior spirit, Nurse Sanders.' Elizabeth nodded in approval and squeezed Connie's arm again.

'How—?'

'Oh news travels fast around here – nothing happens without everyone knowing. Haven't you realised that yet? Yes, Jim overheard – he's always lurking, picking up bits of gossip. I think it makes him feel important. You know what they say about small hands...'

Connie burst out laughing, drawing some distracted glances from the crowd. She scanned, looking for Daisy, but there was no sign of her.

'Oh my!' Elizabeth pointed.

Connie's hand flew to her mouth as she saw that several large crates were heading in the direction of the Nurse's Centre.

'Don't look at Paul.'

Who could obey a command like that? Connie stole a glance at Paul, who was looking at the crates, his mouth a thin line.

'Everyone knows about you standing up to him, and now he looks weak. He won't like that...not at all.'

Connie was oblivious, as she raced after her precious boxes. Ilannaq arrived, equally breathless. 'Wow this is one in the eye for Paul Archer.' She clapped her gloved hands in glee. 'Good for you, Connie.'

There were oohs and ahhs as they discovered scalpels, syringes, various drugs and a secure cabinet to keep them in, plus a logbook to record usage. There were surgical gloves and aprons, basic anaesthetic, forceps, and a range of dressings and bandages. When they were done, Connie sat back pushing her hair behind her ears, and grinned at Ilannaq.

She felt a huge sense of achievement. She had done this! Connie Sanders! With a big helping of understanding from Elizabeth and support from Ilannaq.

As it turned out, Pam had made surprisingly good choices and Connie's shelves were soon stocked with tins of baked beans (Thank you Pam! Did they eat baked beans in Australia?), tinned meat of various types, tinned fruit, tinned vegetables of various kinds, tinned soup, flour, salt, sugar, tinned butter, long-life milk, dried eggs, cocoa, the ubiquitous coffee and even some bars of chocolate. Connie surveyed her hoard wallowing in the sense of ownership. This was her very own food, in her own house, to be cooked and prepared by herself only. She decided to repay Elizabeth and Peter for their kindness and issued an invitation for supper.

She played it safe when they came and produced beans on toast garnished with some labour-intensive strips of spam, the bread heavily laden with tinned butter. It had taken about half an hour to get into the spam tin once the key had snapped, using a strange tin-opening device that Connie had never encountered before. She imagined her mother looking on and tutting impatiently.

Elizabeth and Peter dutifully consumed the meal, pronouncing that it was nothing like they had ever had before. Connie didn't press for more details. The taste of baked beans was a taste of home and she revelled in their warm, sugary caress as Elizabeth praised her bread-making prowess.

'Time for some coffee and a dessert,' announced Elizabeth rummaging in her bag. 'And I've brought biscuits!' She produced them with a flourish. 'Maple syrup cookies.'

'Oh my goodness!' For a few moments they stared reverently at the packet before Elizabeth opened it. And then they inhaled the sugary scent within, closing their eyes and revelling in the moment.

'Where is that coffee, Nurse Sanders? I'm in danger of passing out from exhaustion here,' said Peter as Elizabeth reverently laid the biscuits on a plate.

'Coming right up.' Connie poured three cups from the coffee jug on the stove and they took a cookie each.

'Thank you for sharing these,' Connie said, biting into the soft cookie.

'It's worth it to see your face at this moment,' laughed Elizabeth. 'It wouldn't be the same on our own, would it, Peter?' She looked at her husband who nodded in agreement.

'Some pleasures are best shared, don't you think?' he added.

Connie stopped chewing and felt unexpected tears gathering at the kindness of these two people who she had only known for a few weeks. Taking a sip of coffee, she swallowed hurriedly and looked away.

Connie still hadn't quite got the hang of what time of day, or night, it was. At home, life had generally been arranged around the light of day and the darkness of night, and her body clock was still finding the endless daylight hard to adjust to. Totally reliant on the travel alarm clock that she'd brought with her, Connie learnt that it was 7 a.m. when Ilannaq had appeared at the house, the following morning.

Today they were revisiting Ilannaq's settlement to check on Eshakto, the elderly man with the chest infection. As they approached the village, Connie felt the confidence of a returning visitor, and was grateful for Ilannaq's influence, through her father.

Although the days were still long, it was noticeable that the sun was becoming lower in the sky. Connie had been aware of this over the last few weeks, but out here, in the bay, it was obvious that the light was less brilliant, and the shadow of the canoe had become elongated in the setting sun. Ilannaq had explained that they would only be able to access the village by water for another three or four weeks before the bay started to freeze over. Until the ice became solid enough for skidoos, they would have to travel overland, a much longer and more arduous journey.

Once they had landed and gone through the greetings with Ilannaq's father and the inevitable tea ceremony, Connie was anxious to see her patient. She had tested him and knew he didn't have TB. Having examined him carefully, she had decided to give him a course of antibiotics. They would just have time to return in around a week to see if they had worked. If not, he would need to be airlifted out to Frobisher Bay. Connie saw this as a last resort and didn't want to distress the family. Ilannaq gave Eshakto's daughter careful instructions as to when he needed to take the pills if he was to avoid being airlifted to the hospital and Connie left hoping that when they returned he would have improved.

'Do you have a family back in Manchester?' Ilannaq interrupted Connie's thoughts on the return journey across the water.

'Yes, my parents and my brother, David.' Connie paused.

'I know what that feels like – to be away from everything that you know.'

Connie turned to look at Ilannaq. 'You do?'

'I was one of the children they took away to the mainland. I was in a Canadian school and wasn't even allowed to speak my own language or have any contact with my family.'

Connie couldn't stifle the gasp. 'How old were you?'

'Ten. And I was there until I was fourteen. I have seen flowers, trees and cars,' she added with a wry smile.

'So what makes you want to have anything to do with people like me, never mind help us?'

'It was Rev Brooks who returned me to my people.'

'*Rev Brooks?*'

'Yes. He was visiting the children's home where we were all put. And I was chosen to show him what we were learning because my English was good. I think I charmed him.' Ilannaq gave a mischievous smile. 'Anyway, he was impressed with my English and persuaded the authorities that I could be of more use here, in my own community, as a translator and sort of...go between.'

'And that was okay for you?' Connie was incredulous that this girl's life had been decided for her by white men as if she had been a commodity to be traded.

'Well yes, of course. It meant that I could return to my people and help them understand something of a world most of them have never seen.'

'But don't you hate us?'

'Why should I? Rev Brooks returned me to my people, I have had a better education than I would have had, and most of all, I can speak English,' she said proudly. 'We are a proud people, Connie, but we cannot live separately from the rest of the world.'

Connie digested this in silence, remembering Daisy's last reprimand before she left. 'Grow up, Connie. This world isn't for faint-hearted romantics!'

And do you know one of the best things?' Ilannaq interrupted her thoughts, grinning. 'I get to work with you!'

Once again, tears sprang into Connie's eyes at the unaccustomed kindness. 'Thank you, Ilannaq, and I don't know what I would do without *you*!'

# Chapter Twelve

C onnie spent a warm Saturday in Elizabeth's kitchen where she initiated Connie into the mysteries of cooking with powdered egg, honing her bread-making skills, making cakes and even ice cream, made from evaporated milk. They finished off with a batch of cranberry and blueberry muffins, made with fruit that they had picked themselves. Elizabeth had shown Connie where the berries grew, just outside the settlement, nestled in the frozen tundra enjoying their brief, fragile moment in the Arctic summer.

While they'd been cooking, Connie found herself sharing with Elizabeth something of the disaster of Helen and what had driven her to such a remote place. Elizabeth had said very little, merely tightening her lips and frowning from time to time.

'My mother says I shouldn't wear my heart on my sleeve, that I'm too gullible,' Connie said ruefully as they finished the washing up.

'I wouldn't want to disagree with your mother – she sounds a pretty formidable woman. Maybe you've inherited some of those qualities.'

Connie stopped and thought. It had never occurred to her that she might have inherited anything good from her mother, who, if she was honest, she had been slightly frightened of.

'But I think you also have kindness and empathy, and those qualities have been exploited by Helen in a...shameful way.' Elizabeth had hesitated before finishing the sentence, obviously choosing her words carefully. 'But they are part of who you are, and you need to not let others destroy that side of you. Never go down the road of becoming angry and bitter and not being open to new possibilities.'

Connie felt pieces clicking into place in her head. Maybe she wasn't a stupid person letting people ride roughshod over her, as her mother had suggested, but rather, she had been hurt by Helen because of the very positive characteristics that made her who she was. Elizabeth was right, and Connie pledged to write down her advice and keep it close, vowing she would never lose her natural empathy and kindness. But she knew now that she had to learn how to stop others from taking advantage of who she was.

'When the homesickness hits again, just know that it will never be as bad as the first attack, and that you will come through it. Just recognise it for what it is and let it take its course. I find the best thing is to do something comforting and distracting, like I said before. For me, it's cooking.' She waved her spoon around the kitchen. 'For Peter it's photography.'

'I'm going to miss you so much!' Connie hugged Elizabeth tightly, wishing she never had to let her go. 'You really are my Arctic mother – even if you were a child bride!' They both giggled.

'Okay, enough sermonising. I think we've earnt a drink, and I mean a proper drink.'

This time, Connie recognised almost everybody at Elizabeth and Peter's party and even managed to join in with some of the jokes. The alcohol flowed and everyone seemed in good spirits. Connie tried to bury the fact that she was terrified about Elizabeth leaving, even though she knew that part of her would remain in the form of the advice she had given Connie, now written down and tucked inside her copy of *Great Expectations*. Connie smiled to herself at the irony.

Connie kept cheerful for the whole evening, avoiding too much wine which she knew from past experience would make her maudlin. Instead, she spent some time talking to Peter about photography and cameras. He promised he would send her a suitable camera, along with rolls of film when they were in Frobisher Bay on their brief vacation. He talked again about how to set a photo up and focus on points of interest. Connie soaked everything up, holding on to this as a way of getting through the evening.

The following day, Connie could hardly bring herself to watch Elizabeth, Peter and little Tom, as their kayak reached the plane, which had landed somewhat precariously on a sand bar. She felt Esther's hand slip into her own and she squeezed it firmly as the little family climbed into the plane with one last wave. Connie spoke sternly to herself: 'Okay, pull yourself together, Connie, you've got this far, and this is just the next step in the adventure. This was what you wanted wasn't it? To be able to have stories to tell?' She drew her shoulders back, thought of her mother's strength and lifted her gaze to the Twin Otter banking above them, waving and blowing a kiss.

She turned to see Esther waving, tears in her eyes. Connie hadn't realised how attached Esther had been to little Tom, and he to her. She hadn't known how much time Esther had spent babysitting and minding him until Tom clung to her leg when the time came to say goodbye. 'I want Esther to come too,' he'd cried, burying his face in her coat. Esther had crouched to eye level and reassured him that they would be back before he knew it and to think of all the adventures he would be able to tell her about. Reluctantly, Tom had allowed himself to be coaxed into the canoe and, holding his mother's hand, he had steadfastly continued waving until they had boarded the plane.

Awareness of Daisy's continuing absence over the past few weeks was now turning into anger and confusion. Where was she? It was hard to avoid anyone in a small settlement such as Harbour Inlet, so she had obviously gone somewhere. Connie had ended up going down all too familiar corridors in her thoughts, opening doors as she went. Was it her fault? Had she been too quick to voice her opinions? Was it because she said the wrong things? Would no one ever take her seriously? She always reached the same end point – self-preservation, and she didn't want anything to do with someone, who, yet again, for whatever reason, had abandoned her without explanation. Someone who had the power to make her feel like this. Daisy had too many of Helen's traits and wasn't to be trusted, especially as she was betraying the Inuit by working with the Canadian government. There was no way around it. 'And that's that,' she told herself firmly. As well as a Helen-shaped box, there was now a matching Daisy-shaped box, both lids firmly closed.

Even so, she found herself casually asking François if she knew where Daisy had gone.

She answered, 'But she 'as gone to Frobisher Bay – back to 'er 'offeece. Did she not tell you?'

Connie looked down at her feet to hide her humiliation – and anger – at abandoning her own stern advice so quickly.

François put an arm around her. 'You're sad to lose your friend, no? But I will still be here, and we can still have fun.' She winked mischievously. 'Some films have arrived. They will be shown in the hall, but Rev and Mrs Brooks won't like it and those binoculars will be bizee,' she said in a conspiratorial whisper.

Connie couldn't help laughing. 'That would be wonderful, François, I love films. My mother used to take me to the cinema every Saturday morning.'

'Come and have coffee with me, and we can talk films!'

At that moment, spying the box of reel-to-reel films. François pointed excitedly and mimed a reel-to-reel action. Connie clapped her hands in excitement. 'I love films.'

She called to Esther who had wandered away. 'Isn't this exciting, Esther?'

Esther frowned. 'I'm don't think I'd be allowed to watch films.'

Connie's heart clenched with pity for the girl and made a decision there and then to do her best to include Esther. 'How about I ask your mum if you can come to see one of the films with me?'

Esther couldn't disguise her excitement at the idea. 'Really?'

'Yes, leave it to me. We'll get you in somehow. Now, how is the writing going?' she asked as a distraction, already worrying that she had promised something that she wouldn't be able to deliver.

'Okay, but I haven't done much yet.' Esther wiped her nose of the sleeve of her coat.

'Well, I think this is a good time to get stuck in, don't you? Why not write about today and how it has made you feel?' Connie suggested as they made their way up the beach.

'Yes, I could do that...' Esther hesitated. 'But would it be a bit selfish to just write about myself and my own feelings? Wouldn't it seem a bit...as if I wasn't accepting God's will?'

Connie stopped in her tracks. 'Just because you find something difficult, it doesn't mean you're not accepting it, Esther. It's important to talk and write about how you feel.' She tried not to let the shock sound in her tone.

'But what if the way I feel is sinful?'

Connie was lost for words, well and truly out of her depth in this theological conversation. 'I don't know, but what I can tell you from experience is that it's never good to bottle up your feelings and pretend they're not there.'

'I'm not sure my parents would agree with you,' Esther replied rubbing her toe from side to side in the snow.

'Maybe not, but I believe everyone is entitled to have their own views, and I'm sure your parents have their reasons for thinking as they do. Why not ask them?'

Esther looked at Connie, eyes wide. 'I can't do that.'

'Why not?'

'It would be like...questioning everything we stand for.' Esther drew her arm abruptly away from Connie's and marched off up the track without looking back.

Connie heaved a sigh, wondering if the day could get any worse.

Once the mail had been distributed, and there was no letter, the silence from Daisy started to take on greater significance in spite of Connie's valiant efforts to shut it down. Maybe Daisy wasn't coming back at all and hadn't wanted to say goodbye. No one seemed to know when or if she would return.

'We never know with Daisy,' Jim had told her, with a hint of smug satisfaction. 'She comes and goes in her own time.'

# Chapter Thirteen

The welcome letters from home lifted Connie's spirits and distracted her attention away from the endless circle of her thoughts. She had reread the previous letters many times and they were showing signs of wear and tear. So now, putting on the yellow dressing gown and settling herself with a comforting hot chocolate, Connie read about her father's retirement and other family news. As a skilled engineer, her father had always had work, sometimes travelling as far afield as Faslane to work on nuclear submarines, work he could never talk about. She imagined her father now in the garden shed which he had turned into a fully equipped workshop, tinkering and inventing new gadgets. Connie fondly remembered the bikes he had made for David and her when they were children, always assembled from various spare parts and adapted as they grew older. She smiled as she remembered the family's first car, which only she and David could drive, how he learnt to maintain it – how to take the engine apart and reassemble again, even building an inspection pit in the garage. She knew her father would find plenty to do in his free time, and that her mother would be more than happy that he was occupied in 'the shed.'

She reread several times an uncharacteristic sentence her mother had written – *Whenever I look at the moon, I know that you are looking at the same moon*. She gazed at the moon, casting its luminous light over the bay and thought of her mother – wondering for the first time how she felt now that she and David had left home. Her mother would have had no time for 'snivelling and crying' and 'making a fuss' You just got on with things. So this uncharacteristically emotional sentence made an impact. Connie guessed it was their stoicism and stiff-upper-lip mentality had got them through the war, when her father had been a Bevan Boy, sent down the coal mines by a random lottery draw – his service to the war effort never recognised – and her mother had worked in a munitions factory. If they survived all that, and the bombing of Manchester, Connie could survive this, she told herself sternly. However, that hint of vulnerability from her mother had unsettled her, and she fingered the thin airmail paper, knowing that her mother and father had touched it and maybe even kissed it, allowing the tears to fall freely.

There was even a rare letter from her brother, telling falsely cheerful tales of his life at Sheffield University. She knew him well enough to know that he wasn't entirely happy studying law, but their parents were determined that they should both have 'proper jobs'. Left to his own devices, David would have been happy to get by as a struggling artist, but that had been swiftly ruled out. 'You can always do that as a hobby,' her father had said, 'but it won't earn you any money.'

'And we haven't sent you to that posh grammar school for you to end up on the streets.' His mother had added. This was in spite of the fact that his art teacher had tried to persuade their parents that he was talented and should go to art school. Connie, sighing, felt sad for him. And felt the familiar pangs of homesickness growing,

She remembered Elizabeth's advice and didn't fight the waves as they broke over her. She spent the rest of the evening recording her feelings in a journal she had started. Somehow, when she read it back, she was able to almost stand outside of herself and see her situation more objectively. She looked back at how far she had come, beginning to understand and accept that these feelings were an inevitable part of this adventure. She thought of Thomas Hardy's Tess, and all that she endured, and felt that she would have understood how Connie was feeling. She found herself writing an imaginary conversation she and Tess might have, and became so engrossed that an hour had passed before she knew it. Elizabeth had been right. The trick was not to push the feelings away, but to channel them into some kind of absorbing activity.

When she felt able, a few days later, Connie wrote a long letter to David, attempting to paint in words the landscape and the magnificence of the polar sky: *You would love to paint here, David. The light is amazing...when it's fading as it is now. The red and orange glow from the sun, low in the sky, reflects off the snow and icebergs like some kind of Arctic fire. I always thought of this as a place with no colour – just white, but there are times when it is more vibrant and exhilarating than anything at home. Everything is on a huge canvas and on a such magnificent scale. Who knows, maybe you'll be able to visit sometime.* She also wrote a shorter letter to her parents, reassuring them that she was doing okay – describing some of the work she was doing, and telling her mother about the films they were looking forward to. She wanted them to go on the next plane out, although now that the bay would be freezing soon, it would be easier for the Otter to land, and storms permitting, they might have more regular landings.

There was just time for one more trip across the water to see Eshakto, and Connie was thrilled to see him at the shore waiting for her. His daughter hugged Connie tightly. 'Thank you so much for making him better. We thought he would be taken away from us to hospital,' she said through Ilannaq, although Connie hadn't needed a translation to understand what the young woman was saying.

'This is good,' said Ilannaq. 'Word will spread and people will be happier to get treated.'

Nevertheless, Connie gave Eshakto a thorough examination to be sure and left a further supply of antibiotics should the infection return. They spent some time checking in on the rest of the settlement, and Connie was reassured that most seemed in good health.

On the way back, as they took the last journey she and Ilannaq would make by boat for at least six months, Connie asked Ilannaq to teach her some more basic Inuit – apart from wanting to communicate directly, she also wanted to show that she was making an effort to understand their culture.

Connie mastered *atigi* pronouncing it a-TI-gi, pointing to her coat as Ilannaq nodded in encouragement, followed by *iggaak* – ig-AAK, Inuit for snow goggles. Polar bear, even though she had yet to see one, was *nanuk* – na-NUQ.

'What about "What's wrong?"' Connie asked, thinking of communicating with her patients more directly.

'*Quanikkavit?*' Ilannnaq couldn't hold back her giggles as Connie struggled with the more complicated sounds. 'Qa-nu-IK-ka-vit.' She pronounced it slowly so that Connie could follow the phonetics. Eventually she got it and was determined to practise so that the words would stay in her head. Unlike at school, she now had good reason to learn another language, whereas French had always seemed a bit pointless as she didn't know any French people and had felt it unlikely that she ever would. They finished the lesson with numbers: *atausiq* – one, Connie carefully emphasising the middle syllable, *marruuk* – two, and *pingasut* – three, at which point she felt her brain was full to overflowing.

Ilannaq grinned. 'This is why they accept you, because you make an effort to understand our way of life...and eat our food,' she added, teasing. Connie resolutely turned her thoughts away from anything to do with eyes. 'A lot of Westerners don't – they think we should learn their way of life instead and forget our own.'

Connie remembered about Ilannaq's time in the government school and put her hand on her arm. 'I'm so sorry, Ilannaq.'

'It's okay, it's worked out okay now. And Rev Brooks is making the Bible into Inuit and some Christian songs, so it is better for us.'

Connie had her doubts about the motivation behind Rev Brooks's work. In her mind it seemed a devious way of undermining Inuit culture and inserting Christianity.

As they neared Harbour Inlet, Connie wished she'd had a camera. A thin, flexible, layer of ice had already formed on the water, and the undulating movement caught the light of the setting sun, like a sparkling curtain of light billowing across the bay. She tried to capture the moment in her mind as the thin ice shimmered in oranges and reds as it moved between already forming pieces of thicker ice.

Once they were ashore, the first flakes of snow started to flurry around them as they beached the canoe. The romantic in Connie revelled in the moment and could have stood, taking in the scene for some time. However, Ilannaq, ever practical, informed Connie that it was now time for her to master the art of riding a skidoo, saying with a grin. 'Don't worry, it's easy.'

As September progressed, the sun made its way slowly but surely towards the horizon, reminding Connie of an all-day version of the winter-afternoon light at home. The landscape took on a vaguely eerie quality, a premonition of the darkness to come. And when the snow started to arrive in earnest, Connie hadn't been prepared for the howling, bitter, winds that herded the freezing flakes of snow and ice before them, making everything a mask of white. So different from the initial, gentle, exciting snowfall she had experienced a few days earlier, and back at home. And the cold...it was unlike anything Connie had ever experienced, a chill that went right to the core of her. Ilannaq had reassured her, laughing. 'This is only minus 10, wait 'til it's minus 30!'

Connie had been told that the most effective clothes were those of Inuit origin – highly coloured parkas with zips for the women and pull-on styles for the men. These were generally made from animal skins and were highly decorated – most Inuit women, like Ilannaq's mother, being skilful embroiderers. Then there were the outer parkas, made of Grenfell cloth, which were water- and wind-proof, and also decorated with brightly coloured embroidered designs. The two parkas, when worn together, provided protection from any kind of Arctic weather. Connie learnt from Ilannaq that the Inuit could identify which area they were each from by the shape of their parka hoods: those in the eastern Arctic were pointed, whereas the western Arctic Inuit had rounded hoods. Connie soon acquired an outer parka from the Bay store and was more than glad of the investment – it would, along with the thermals, become her best friend.

By now, she was used to wearing *kamiks*, the soft soled boots made from seal or caribou skin, lined with fur which were surprisingly comfortable, and specifically designed for the cold, dry weather of the Arctic winter. But now they really came into their own. She had learnt that this footwear was designed to enable Inuit hunters to be agile and approach their prey in silence. Connie had learnt to store her *kamiks* on the outer porch rather than follow her natural instinct to take them in and dry them out. Ilannaq explained that if they dried they would stiffen and become unwearable, and that then the skin had to be chewed by the women to soften it again. Connie put that image out of her head and was glad of the more contemporary skidoo boots for wetter conditions.

One morning, suitably attired, Connie set off to take some photos of the bay, using a camera that Peter had kindly left for her to practise on, aiming to capture a sense of the low sun on the ice and snow, and the wavy ice she had seen from the boat. In the week or so since she had seen it, however, the phenomenon had disappeared, the ice was now too thick and solid to move. She focused instead on the contrast between light and shade, aiming to capture some of the long shadows cast by the mountains. She was especially pleased with one shot of her own shadow stretching across the ice into the bay. She felt it was an apt depiction of the amplified presence of one small, isolated, person in this magnificent landscape.

Beginning to feel the inevitable cold, even through her Inuit clothing, Connie was heading home when she met François coming out of the Bay store.

'I have just taken Thierry some lunch. Is this a good time for coffee and film talk?'

'That would be just the thing. Thanks François.' Connie was looking forward to getting to know François better, and now, relishing the thought of some delicious French coffee, it seemed just the time.

Connie slowly divested herself of some of her outer clothing. The *kamiks*, in particular, had taken a long time to get out of now that they were damp from the snow. François laughed, saying, 'It will get easier. There is, how do you say it, a...' she looked at the ceiling, searching for the word.

'Knack?'

'Yes, a knack.'

François made coffee and laid out some pastries on a plate.

'You made these?'

'Yes, they are not as good as real French ones, but they are good enough.' François grinned.

Connie took a bite and nodded her head as she chewed and swallowed. 'Oh my. You must teach me how to make them.'

'They take quite a time to make, but I have nothing else to do, so...' François didn't finish the sentence, and Connie felt a pang of sympathy for her, wondering how she spent her days. 'But you...you are busy with a job. If you like, I can make you some.'

'Oh, François, that would be wonderful. Thank you.'

'Did you hear that those stupid people in Frobisher Bay did not send the projector with the films? We have to wait for the next flight. *Zut alors*!' François threw her hands in the air in frustration.

'No I hadn't heard. We'll just have to make do with talking about films then.' Connie finished the pastry, licking her fingers, and refused a second. 'I'm pacing myself. Maybe in a bit?'

'So what is your favourite film?'

Connie cast her mind back to the Saturday morning films she had seen with her mother. 'That's so hard to answer, I liked *Casablanca*, the *Dam Busters*...anything with Elizabeth Taylor or Audrey Hepburn. Oh, and Bette Davis, of course.'

François squealed. 'I love Audrey Hepburn, she is so *chique*! Have you seen *Breakfast at Tiffany's*?'

'I loved that. And *My Fair Lady*!'

'Those costumes are to die for.' Connie laughed at François's theatrical gesture.

'But one of my real favourites is *Gone with the Wind*.'

'Oh my God, yes. Clark Gable.'

'And Vivien Leigh!'

'And National Velvet with Elizabeth Taylor. I cried buckets over that.' The memories came flooding back, and before Connie knew it a couple of hours had passed and several more pastries had been consumed. Eventually, she stood to go. 'Thank you so much, François. I have so enjoyed this afternoon.'

'You are welcome, and so have I. Let's do it again soon, and let's hope the projector arrives. We have Elvis Presley to watch!'

'Here, put them on like this.' François showed Connie how to put on the damp *kamiks* in one swift movement.

Connie did a poor imitation, and laughing said, 'I think I need to practise.'

As she walked home, Connie reflected on how, for a few hours, she had been able to lose herself with François, in the warm world of films, briefly forgetting the gathering darkness and growing chill of the weather outside. She began to under-stand how François so enjoyed being enveloped in a cloak of glamour and romance, a way of coping with the challenges of Arctic life.

# Chapter Fourteen

Ilannaq had not been wrong about the skidoo. Once Connie had summoned up the energy to pull the starter cord and turn the engine over, riding was quite easy. It was something like a cross between a tricycle and a moped, and much more stable than Connie had imagined. Two skis at the front were controlled by handlebars and at the back, under a passenger seat and a storage box was a sturdy caterpillar track which propelled the machine forwards. Ilannaq, laughing at her modern skidoo boots purchased from the Bay store, had warned her to be careful of soft snow, and not to turn the handlebars too suddenly.

Returning to the Nurse's Station with a new shipment, Connie revelled in the freedom and ease of getting around, although Ilannaq had warned her not to venture too far alone, and certainly not without a few torches, as the Bombardier skidoos had no lights. Connie found this strange in a vehicle that had been designed for the Arctic winter when it was mostly dusk or dark. A parcel from Peter containing the promised camera along with several rolls of film and a book about basic photography had arrived on the same flight. Connie was touched at his kindness and put the package carefully into the storage compartment – a special treat to look forward to.

She had almost reached the Nurse's Centre when Daisy appeared, as if from nowhere, in front of her, forcing Connie to slide to an awkward stop.

'God, Daisy! What do you think you're doing?' Connie's anger spilled out before she had a chance to moderate it.

'Well, look at you, skidoo rider extraordinaire!' When Connie didn't answer, Daisy came closer. 'I'm sorry, Connie.'

'For nearly giving me a heart attack, or for leaving without saying goodbye? Or maybe for helping to destroy what you said was important. Or maybe for being so damned patronising!' Connie remounted the skidoo, intending to ride off before any further unintended words came out of her mouth.

'Both. All of it,' said Daisy, putting her hand on Connie's arm. 'I'm sorry to have gone off like that... I just...look could I come round later? I want to try and put things right.'

Connie moved her arm away. 'I don't think that's a good idea, do you? Let's just leave things for now.' She restarted the skidoo.

'Look, I know you're upset with me and with good reason. It was rude of me to say what I did and flounce off like a sulky teenager.'

Connie couldn't stifle a laugh at the image of Daisy as a teenager doing silly teenagerish things. Surely that was more her own territory.

'Okay, I suppose I could just allow you five minutes to finish your apology over a drink.' Connie spoke with mock-severity, the anger and hurt she had been battling over the last few weeks, evaporating as if a spell had been cast by Daisy's presence.

They sat in silence looking out over the developing ice, red and pink in the dying light, with bowls of ice cream. Deciding that hot drinks could wait, Connie had felt that somehow the occasion demanded the sugar rush of ice cream, and Daisy had been only too happy to comply.

'Mmm, this is heaven,' Daisy said, leaning her head back against the settee as she swallowed. 'Chef Elizabeth has taught you well, Nurse Sanders.'

Even though her anger had thawed, it hadn't completely disappeared, and Connie didn't reply, wanting more of an apology from Daisy.

Eventually, it came: 'Connie, I'm sorry, I really am for going off like that. I should have said goodbye and told you where I was going.'

Connie continued to focus on the view, as Daisy leant back on the settee, clasped her hands behind her head and closed her eyes.

'Is that it? So that apology is supposed to put everything right? The way you just took off, as if you couldn't get away from me fast enough?' Connie couldn't keep the heat of her returning anger out of her voice – anger at Daisy's casual dismissal of her feelings.

'What makes you think I was running away from you? Not everything is about you, Connie.'

Connie looked at the floor. This friendship wasn't going to work. What else was there to say? She knew for sure now – glad that there were no lingering doubts.

As Connie stood to put the bowls in the sink, Daisy spoke.

'You talk about me running away, but what about you? What are *you* running away from?'

'What are you talking about? I'm here to do a job. It looked interesting, so I applied for it and here I am.'

'No, but why are you *really* here?' Daisy seemed unconscious of the hostility in Connie's tone, or maybe she was just ignoring it. 'Most of us incomers are here for a reason other than our jobs. Most of us are running away from something –

like me, and especially the draft-dodgers at the Hudson Bay. So what are *you* running away from, Connie?'

'I'm not running away. I told you. Some of us just want to live a bit and do some good at the same time.'

'As opposed to the boring and un-useful life you had at home?'

'Something like that.' Connie wasn't going to share any of her thoughts about Helen with Daisy. From what she knew so far about the sort of person Daisy was, she never would.

'Oh come on, Connie, unwind a bit. You don't have to be all stiff and frosty with me.'

'Don't I?'

The words were out of Connie's mouth before she could check her anger.

Without answering, Daisy stood and headed for the door, tugging the red hat down over her wild blonde hair. Something about that movement made Connie soften a little inside, but she was careful not to show it.

'Right, I'm off. Paperwork to do.' But just as she was heading out of the door, and Connie felt she could breathe again, Daisy turned. 'Would you fancy coming on a day out with me at some point...to see some ice, snow, and other white things?'

Connie hesitated.

'Don't worry, I promise you'll be safe with me.' Daisy gave her a steady look. 'I'll take that as a yes, then. Let me know where and when.'

'*What?* I—'

What was it about Daisy that made it so difficult to say no?

The flight had also delivered the returning teachers, Kathy and Tom, who were welcomed back as old friends, this being their third stint in Harbour Inlet. There was undisguised envy that they spent three months every summer in the south, missing the mosquitos, but they took the teasing in good part.

It turned out that Kathy and Tom were from Hampshire. At home, Connie had heard dark tales about southerners and how snobbish and hostile they were, but she determined to keep an open mind. Here in the great expanse of the Arctic, English provincial thinking somehow seemed trivial and irrelevant.

They had wasted no time in inviting everyone round for drinks, obviously curious about Connie – a fellow Brit. Connie found it a challenge to adjust to the house having such a different atmosphere. But was hard to identify, as, like Kathy and Tom, Elizabeth and Peter had loved entertaining, but there was something...

'So, what do you think of the place so far?' enquired Tom, leaning back in the chair and crossing his legs, with a wry smile.

'It's taken a bit of getting used to, but I'm still here,' Connie replied, having a sense that she was being assessed rather than simply accepted for who she was.

Tom nodded. 'It's surprising what dark things live suspended in a frozen landscape. Maybe you haven't encountered them yet.'

Connie looked at him, unsure how to respond. 'What do you mean?'

Kathy appeared with more wine. The moment had passed, and the subject was obviously closed. Connie tried to ignore a nagging feeling that something wasn't right here. What had he meant? Dark things suspended in a frozen landscape? She had covered up so many of her own feelings over the years that the comment seemed to strike a chord.

Connie was still pondering on Tom's cryptic remark when there was a great commotion. Tom and Kathy rushed to the front door just in time to catch an older Inuit man as he pitched forward onto the floor.

'Elijah, what in God's name are you up to?'

'You party. Me join in,' was his drunken reply.

With a hand each under Elijah's arms, Tom and Paul dragged his heavy weight into the room.

Tom laughed. 'Elijah usually joins us at some point in the proceedings!'

A glass of beer in hand, and speaking rapidly in Inuktitut, Elijah produced a number of carvings from his pockets, apparently as gifts for Tom and Kathy. They selected one or two and gently returned the rest to Elijah's pockets.

Tom seemed right at home with the Hudson Bay drinkers, and soon he, Thierry, Elijah, Jim and Paul were engrossed in a heavy-duty drinking game. Kathy and François seemed deep in conversation while also consuming generous amounts of alcohol, and every so often a shriek of laughter would erupt. Connie guessed they had a lot to catch up on.

Feeling increasingly uncomfortable, her old fear of being on the edge of things and not part of the inner circle threatening to take over, Connie made her excuses and left as soon as she could. This party was only going one way...

Back in the peace of her own home, Connie realised how noisy the gathering had been, and how the alcohol had flowed. She felt uncomfortable about the incident with Elijah, she thought that the way Kathy and Tom had treated him was somehow demeaning as they had laughed at him. And since when had the Inuit had Western, Biblical names? She couldn't have imagined any of that happening on Elizabeth's watch, and Connie felt her absence as a tightness settled in her chest.

With each day, the sun was sinking lower in the sky, and Connie was determined to take some more photos while natural daylight still remained. She spent time reading the instruction book and trying out new settings on her camera. Conscious that she would have to make the rolls of film last, she was hesitant about her first few experimental shots, but once she got over the initial nervousness, she took several photos around Harbour Inlet, trying to capture the pre-darkness atmosphere and convey some narrative. With the permission of several of the Inuit, who were in awe of the black machine that could reflect them back – they had already seen the developed photos that Peter had taken – Connie focused on capturing the women preparing pelts and skins, embroidering delicate and beautiful designs, as well as those Inuit who were skilled carvers.

She watched, entranced, as an elderly Inuit man patiently showed a boy, who Connie guessed would have been about Esther's age, how to carefully sand down a carving of a seal. The form was already there, carved out of the stone, and now it needed a polish with sandpaper to put the finishing touches. The older man worked with the sandpaper, looking at the boy with sharp glances to make sure he was watching and that he understood the motion. When he put the seal into the boy's hands and passed him the sandpaper, Connie could sense the child's nervousness. Maybe this was the first time he had been allowed to help. With tentative strokes he brushed the sandpaper over the stone, and looked at the older man, who gestured for him to use more force, miming an energetic action with his arm. Connie took several shots, capturing these special moments for ever. Maybe the boy was the old man's grandson, or maybe some other relative. The romantic Connie (who was still very much alive) wondered if she was seeing the first attempts of a master carver of the future.

Soon the boy was sanding with intense concentration, occasionally looking up to see the older man nod in approval, as he eventually returned to his own work, carving a piece of bone with a small hammer and chisel. Connie could see the beginnings of a figure emerging and guessed that it might be a hunter. She had learnt that the Inuit made carvings of what was around them, often of animals and fish, hunters, igloos or depictions of hunting expeditions. Sometimes they would depict the shamen having heroic adventures against evil beings. Connie could have spent hours watching the master and his apprentice at work, but eventually had to drag herself away, leaving with an appreciative smile and a clap in their direction.

As she was passing what she still thought of as Elizabeth's house, Kathy opened the door and shouted. 'Hello Connie, fancy a coffee?'

Connie, reluctant to break the spell of the last few hours, hesitated. But she didn't want to offend Kathy, and so accepted the offer.

'Did you enjoy last night? I'm so sorry if we made you feel left out, it was just so good to see everyone again. Still adjusting from the home counties world though.'

'You could always visit the Brooks's for a flavour.' Connie couldn't help herself. 'And yes, thanks for inviting me.'

Kathy flung back her head and laughed. 'You're so right. We usually get an invite for lunch on our return, so I'll make the most of it when we go, although I can't stand cricket,' she whispered conspiratorially. 'So where are you from? I'm guessing somewhere north of Watford?'

Connie tamped down the reflex response to bristle at such a comment, remembering her earlier thought that petty grievances from home didn't belong here. 'Manchester, actually,' she answered.

'Isn't that where Jim comes from?' said Kathy as she poured the coffee.

'Yes...' Connie couldn't think how to continue the sentence tactfully, as she didn't know what Kathy and Tom's relationship with him might be. She had learnt to be more cautious before opening her mouth.

'Say no more,' Kathy said, a conspiratorial tone in her voice. 'We call him "Wandering-hands Jim". He tries it on with all the women.'

Relaxing, Connie smiled. 'But don't tar all of us Mancunians with the same brush.' She couldn't resist the dig.

'I wouldn't dream of it. We have our share of WH Jim's down south as well.'

Taking a few sips of coffee, Kathy leant forward, elbows on the table. 'I hear you've had a few run-ins with Paul Archer...' She waited expectantly for Connie to respond.

Feeling on safer ground but remembering the camaraderie around the alcohol from the night before, Connie hesitated.

As if reading her thoughts, Kathy patted her hand. 'Don't be fooled by last night. There's no love lost between Tom and Paul...or Jim, for that matter. But when there are few drinking companions to be had, needs must.' She grinned at Connie's confused expression. 'And he believes in the old adage – keep your friends close and your enemies closer. So...about Paul...'

'Well, he hasn't made it easy for me, that's for sure. But I think I'm getting the measure of him.' Connie stopped, wondering if she'd said too much.

'Don't let him bully you. It sounds as if you've already made a good start standing up to him.'

Connie wondered what else people had been saying about her but wasn't going to embarrass herself by asking.

As they chatted about Kathy and Peter's visit home over the summer, Connie was able to keep the waves of homesickness at bay. Their lives seemed a far cry from her own world in Manchester. Apparently, they had spent the summer visiting relatives and family who lived in large houses in the countryside. Drinks parties and dinners had played a large part in the many social gatherings, along with a few trips to the opera at a place called Glyndebourne, a performance which needed to be preceded by a lavish outdoor picnic, complete with candelabra and white tablecloths, it seemed. Connie felt on safe ground – definitely not her world.

'Your family sound very different to mine.' Connie couldn't help herself.

'I guess it comes with the territory of being the daughter of a duke,' Kathy said, casually.

Connie opened her mouth but couldn't think of anything to say and abruptly closed it again, as her cheeks reddened.

'I know. It's weird, isn't it? But I can only cope with that life for a few months every year before I start to feel claustrophobic. I always enjoy getting back to the Arctic.'

Maybe the north/south divide did still exist here in one of the most far-flung corners of the world, after all. Connie was struck by the thought that if she had spent the summer in Kathy and Tom's world, she would probably have felt just as homesick and out of place as she did here. How could such a small country as theirs contain so many worlds? And what had brought Kathy and Tom to this remote settlement, of all places? Connie remembered Daisy's words about her fellow settlers: 'Most of us are running from something.'

Breaking into Connie's thoughts, Kathy stood up, taking the cups to the sink. 'Changing the subject – when the sea-lift came in, do you know if any butter came?'

'I had butter, and I think everyone else did too...' Connie said, cautiously.

'Because we've got hardly any!'

'I think Elizabeth did quite a bit of cooking before she went...'

'I knew it! I knew she'd used it all up. That was supposed to be a year's supply!' Kathy threw up her hands in exasperation.

For the second time, Connie could think of nothing useful to say, and made a hasty exit.

# Chapter Fifteen

Taking the last chance, while daylight remained, to visit some of the far-flung settlements, Daisy invited Connie to come with her. 'I promised you a white day out.' She grinned.

After some initial reluctance on Connie's part, Daisy had talked her round, and they had eventually set off in high spirits. Connie, in spite of her misgivings, was excited to be venturing further into this white wilderness. She had made sure to bring the camera and an extra roll of film.

They travelled for a long time in silence, Connie following the tracks of Daisy's skidoo, passing giant rosy pink mountains of snow, which cast long grey shadows over the ground ahead of them. The sheer vastness of this multicoloured wilderness was hard to comprehend, and Connie was aware of herself and Daisy, speeding along, mere specks in the landscape.

After a while, Daisy stopped and killed her engine. Connie followed suit. 'I thought you could do with a rest. We've covered quite a distance.'

Suddenly aware of her aching joints and the sudden stillness after the jolting movement of the speedy skidoo, Connie had to agree. 'I was so busy looking at everything, I didn't notice.' She stood and stretched her aching back and walked on the spot, drawing her knees up to her chest, or at least, as far as her bulky clothing would allow.

Daisy laughed. 'An interesting movement, Nurse Sanders.' She followed suit and they walked on the spot with high strides until Connie collapsed onto the skidoo, laughing.

'How do you know where we're going?' Connie spoke once they had got their breath back.

'I follow the sun and watch for landmarks. See that pile of rocks over there? That's how I know we're getting close. The settlement is a few miles north-west of here.'

Daisy poured a welcome hot drink from a flask she produced from her skidoo carrier. 'Never say I don't know how to treat a girl,' she said as they knocked their cups together.

Connie laughed but was disconcerted by the comment. What had Daisy meant? It sounded almost as if they were on some kind of date – here in the Arctic wilderness. How many people would have been on a date like this? She put the thought from her mind and changed the subject.

'I went to have drinks with Kathy and Tom the other night...' she left the sentence hanging.

'A bit different from Elizabeth and Peter, yes? What did you make of Lady Kathy?'

'She's okay, and friendly – a bit out of my experience though. And Elizabeth's certainly in her bad books for using all the butter.'

'I don't think Elizabeth will lose any sleep over that.' Daisy laughed.

'I can't put my finger on it, but it just didn't feel the same as when Elizabeth and Peter had everyone round. Everyone was drinking just as much as usual, and Kathy and Tom are really good hosts, but...'

Daisy turned to face Connie. 'But?'

'I didn't like the way they treated Elijah. It was almost like they encouraged him to get drunk and then made fun of him. And he gave them some carvings, like they were nothing. But I've seen how much work goes into making those.' Connie paused. 'I don't think Kathy and Tom should have taken them, just like that.'

Daisy's brow creased into a frown. 'You're right. They shouldn't have taken those. They are beautiful pieces of art, and because people like us just take them when they are offered, the Inuit don't realise their value.'

'Why don't they sell them?'

'Who to? The outside world probably doesn't know anything about them, and the white people just accept them and don't really value them either. Although, I have heard that some of the Hudson Bay men and government officials have been selling pieces when they are on the mainland.'

'Government officials like Paul Archer?'

Daisy shrugged 'I wouldn't be surprised.'

'And they're keeping the money?'

'Yup. That's what I've heard.'

'This isn't right.'

As they finished their drinks, Connie was, once more, overwhelmed by the silent, still landscape, but then there was something in the distance and she held her breath as the movement of a polar bear distinguished it from the white camouflage, around a hundred yards away. Daisy turned and slowly picked up the hunting rifle from behind her.

'What are you...?'

She waved at Connie to be quiet, and they watched, transfixed as the bear carried on along its path, seemingly oblivious to their presence. Every so often it stopped, sniffing the air. Connie cursed herself for not having the camera ready, but it was too late now, so she sat and watched, pinching herself that she, Connie Sanders was here in the middle of the Arctic watching a polar bear. She whispered 'Hello, *Nanuk*,' under her breath.

Eventually it disappeared. 'Oh...' was all she could breathe out, in a cloud of condensation. They sat in silence.

'Sorry to scare you with the gun, but wild animals are un-predictable and a polar bear could kill you with one swipe of its paw.' Daisy brought her back down to earth with a jolt.

'Would you really have shot it?' Connie had to ask.

'If it was a question of us or it – yes. But it would be unusual for it to approach us.'

Connie got out the camera and took some shots, deter-mined to record the moment even if the star of the show was no longer on the stage. Gradually, she became aware of the cold numbing her legs and feet, even through the insulation of her parka and skidoo boots, and in a strangely unsettling moment felt unable to move.

'I know. This is how the cold gets to you eventually. Come on, we'd better get going. We're nearly there.' Daisy seemed to have read her thoughts.

The settlement was very similar to those Connie had al-ready visited, but without the comforting presence of Ilannaq she felt apprehensive. However, word had travelled of her healing powers, and they were greeted with smiles...and tea.

She had seen that the residents seemed to be in good health and having carried out the required vaccinations, Connie was ready to leave. Daisy, however, was deep in conversation with the elder in fluent Inuktitut. Now able to understand the odd word, but not enough to follow the conversation, Connie waited patiently gazing at a bunch of plastic roses and carnations in a vase. She had noticed these colourful blooms in many of the homes she had visited and recalled Ilannaq's observation that she had 'actually seen' real flowers and trees. Most of these Inuit households make do with plastic look-alikes, and Connie tried to imagine never having seen the countryside and her father's precious roses in their Manchester back garden.

Eventually, Daisy beckoned her over and explained the animated conversation. 'I remembered what you said about Elijah and the Inuit carvings, and I was asking Hanta here whether they would be interested in selling them to interested Westerners for a fair price.'

'And?' Connie glanced at Hanta who gave a vigorous nod in her direction.

'I've said we will find out what would be a fair price and where they could be sold.'

'We will?'

'Well, *I* will, when I next go to the mainland. What do you think?'

'I think it would have been nice to be consulted beforehand, so I could have joined in the conversation.'

Daisy looked down at the floor. 'I thought you would be pleased. Pleased that I'm doing something to celebrate the Inuit culture – that I'm not totally the Western baddie that you think I am.'

Connie felt her heart soften and wondered once again why she couldn't stay angry with Daisy for long, when she was with her.

They became aware of Hanta and his family watching this interaction with worried faces, so Daisy turned and said something that made the smiles return.

'I told them that we both want to help them, and that we just needed to sort a few things out between us.'

Connie raised her eyebrows and smiled at the assembled company and for some reason found herself shaking Daisy's hand to which everyone clapped and cheered.

'Okay. That's that sorted then...partner.' Daisy spoke with a laugh in her voice.

They set off on the endless white, grey and blue journey home. Connie insisting on stopping every so often to capture on film the immense grey and purple shadows of the mountains, thrilled to capture a couple of young Arctic foxes romping in the snow. She wasn't sure if the light was right but was happy to experiment anyway.

They reached Harbour Inlet just as darkness descended.

'Thank you so much for today, Daisy.' Connie turned as they arrived at her house.

'I glad you enjoyed it.' Daisy paused, shifting on the seat of her skidoo. 'Am I forgiven?'

Connie reflected for a moment and found that the fire of her anger had lost its power during the day, and had now reduced to pale embers. 'It seems so.'

As Daisy heaved an over-dramatic sigh, the last of the pale embers disappeared and Connie found herself laughing. 'I guess it's time for a hot chocolate.' As Daisy readily dismounted from the skidoo. Connie added, 'And I have other goodies.'

Daisy's eyes widened. 'You are such a tease, Nurse Sanders.'

'Of the edible kind,' Connie added hastily.

'Of course, what else?'

Once they were settled watching the ice sheet growing across the bay as it glimmered in the twilight, they munched on François's pastries and sipped hot chocolate. 'What more could you want for after a white day?' Daisy hummed in appreciation.

'I know. Aren't these amazing?'

'She could sell these in the Bay shop.'

Connie sat up. 'That's a brilliant idea, Daisy. I'll suggest it to her.' She wondered if supplying the Bay shop with fresh baked goods would give more purpose to François's days.

After a silence as they savoured François's handiwork, Connie said, 'I'm so envious of your Inuktitut skills. I really need to learn more than the odd word.'

'I guess I've just picked it up over time – and you will too. And you've got Ilannaq, what would she do if you spoke fluent Inuktitut?'

This thought hadn't occurred to Connie and for a moment she was worried.

'I'm only joking! You'll most likely always need Ilannaq, she is indispensable for many reasons, not just because she is an interpreter.'

Connie sat up, becoming aware of movement in the sky. It was if the darkness was shimmering – a curtain blowing in the breeze in the heavens. She stood and went to the window. 'Oh my goodness. Is that...?'

'It's the aurora borealis – the northern lights to you and me. Come outside and you'll get a better view.'

Could this day get any better? Daisy grabbed Connie's hand, but she was only just conscious of it as she stood, breathless, looking out over the bay. 'I've seen pictures of this, but isn't it usually coloured, like purples and yellows?'

'Yes, in photos, but with the naked eye, it's mostly like this.' They watched in silence as the show unfolded before them. Pale waves chasing each other across the sky, and curtains rippling through the heavens. Connie stood very still, feeling that if she moved, the show would be over and the moment ruined.

After a while Connie remembered to breathe, quietly so as not to disturb the moment. It was the most magnificent, most silent show she had ever seen. The only accompaniment was the occasional creaking of the ice as it grew a cover across the waters of the bay. For the second time in a day, she felt truly insignificant as nature danced before her. When at last the curtain had fallen on the shimmering skies, Connie rubbed her aching neck.

'I need to learn to take photos of this. I'll write to Peter for advice.'

Once they were seated back in the warmth with refilled drinks. Connie turned to Daisy. 'So what's the plan with the carvings?'

Daisy was suddenly business-like. 'Okay, I'm going back to Frobisher Bay next week— I was going to tell you,' she added hastily.

Connie smiled.

'Anyway, while I'm there I'll do a bit of research about whether there is a market for the carvings and if they're being sold, where, and for how much. Oh, and about the names, the Brooks like to give converts biblical names – another way of denying Inuit culture! And before you say anything – that's not our battle to fight.'

Connie laughed in spite of her indignation. 'You're getting to know me too well.' And immediately felt cross with herself for relenting so easily. Daisy hadn't seemed to notice, and was already putting on her outer clothes, so she moved swiftly on.

'Good plan to find out more about selling the carvings.' Even so, Connie couldn't help asking the next question: 'How long will you be gone?'

'Probably several weeks, maybe a month or so. I have to prepare and present reports for the government at a conference in Montreal. I need to be very persuasive!'

'I'll miss you...' Connie leant forward and hugged Daisy. When Daisy didn't return the hug with the same enthusiasm,

Connie cursed her treacherous, impulsive nature, and tried to lighten the moment: 'Oh, and could you get me some more rolls of 35mm film? Colour and black and white?'

'Yes, Ma'am.' Daisy saluted, turning to pull her boots on, and Connie felt a falling sensation in the pit of her stomach. But then Daisy turned and held Connie's hands firmly, holding her gaze. 'I'll miss you too.'

And then she was gone.

# Chapter Sixteen

K nowing in advance that Daisy was going away and that they were working on a joint venture together, somehow made her absence less painful this time, although she would always leave a Daisy-shaped space in Connie's mind when she wasn't around, and she missed her enthusiasm and energy.

As Connie dragged her gaze away from the Twin Otter circling and heading off to Frobisher Bay, she realised that someone was talking to her.

'Someone special on that plane, huh?' The tall, gangly young man standing beside her turned and held out his hand. 'Oliver.'

Connie warmed to his open and frank face, still boyish with a smattering of freckles. He reminded her of her brother, David.

'Uh, yes, sorry. Connie.' She shook his hand.

'Looks like you need something to take your mind off whoever just took your heart with them on that Otter. So, what is there to do around here?' His deep-south accent reminded Connie of *Gone with the Wind* and she smiled.

'Well, we could go out for some lunch and then maybe go clubbing later, if you're up for it.' Connie felt something of her old, fun-loving self.

'Okay, but in the absence of coffee shops and clubs...'

François bounced up, her eyes shining. '*Bonjour*. You must be Oliver! Thierry said you were coming to work at the Hudson Bay. You have brought a ray of sunshine with you.'

Oliver looked doubtfully at the lowering clouds that had gathered since the flight took off, and then back at François. 'Oh you mean *me*?'

'Not you, *ma chérie*, although I'm sure you will be a ray of sunshine. No, I mean, the projector – it has come! Stupid idiots, sending the films with no projector last time. You must both come tonight to see Elvis. Thierry will know how to work the projector. Come at 7.30.' She jumped up and down in excitement. 'Come, Oliver, Thierry will show you where you are living.' She linked her arm through Oliver's and steered him away.

Oliver threw a mock-scared look over his shoulder, and Connie couldn't help giggling. She had never seen François so animated.

As she turned to return to the Nurse's Station, Esther came running towards her, loping in great, long strides. Breathless, she caught hold of Connie's arm, her eyes shining with excitement. 'I'm coming to the film. I've asked my mother and she says it's okay to come.'

Connie tried to hide her surprise. 'Really? Are you sure? Did you tell her it was an Elvis Presley film?'

Esther nodded vigorously, hopping from foot to foot in excitement. 'I'll meet you at the hall at 7 o'clock.'

'Right you are. I'll wait for you by the door.' Maybe Mrs Brooks was having a change of heart about keeping Esther closeted in such a narrow world.

By 7.15, the church hall was full, with standing space only. The early birds who started arriving at 6.30 had quickly filled the chairs. There was a buzz of excitement from Westerners and Inuit, alike in anticipation of the treat to come. There was no need for blackout curtains as it was almost dark outside. At 7.30 Thierry strode to the front where a screen, cleverly constructed out of old sheets by François, stood – a blank canvas waiting to be filled with colour and movement.

'Welcome to the Harbour Inlet Cinema.'

This statement was greeted with rapturous applause.

'I give you Elvis Presley!' And with a flourish he strode back to the projector.

After a few crackles and fuzzy images, the title appeared on the screen, *Jailhouse Rock*. There were gasps of amazement at the moving pictures and music from many of the Inuit who had never seen TV, never mind the big screen.

Connie felt Esther grab her arm in excitement. 'Oh, I love it already!' Connie squeezed her hand, enjoying the girl's excitement.

Connie, aware of Oliver on her other side, looked at him and grinned. 'If we can't go clubbing this is the next best thing.'

But just as the title music was getting into full swing, the images blurred and the sound slithered down as the film ground to a halt. Consternation filled the hall. Some of the Inuit, thinking that that had been the full show got up to leave.

'Come on, Thierry! What're you playing at?' yelled Paul.

Thierry good-naturedly waved a hand as he delved into the mechanics of the projector, and after a few minutes, the film resumed.

Connie hadn't realised how much she had missed music and was itching to get up and dance. She thought again of her mother and their Saturday cinema outings, although she wasn't sure what she would have made of Elvis Presley.

When the final song started, Connie was on her feet, along with Oliver, dusting off her best dance steps. The excitement was contagious and soon Paul Archer had followed suit, demonstrating the most amazing jive steps that Connie had ever seen, along with François. For a brief spell, his face was alight with the music, and she felt she was seeing a glimpse of a Paul Archer that was rarely allowed to surface. Inuit dancers joined in with the party atmosphere, their smiles wide. The clapping went on for several minutes after the music had stopped and everyone seemed reluctant to leave the hall to go out into the darkness.

'Come on, party girl, let's get you home.' Connie put her arm around Esther.

'That was amazing. Will you teach me to dance? I want to learn the jive!'

'François might be your best bet in that department, but we'll see.'

'You've certainly got a little follower there,' said Oliver grinning, as Esther was already making a beeline for François.

Connie didn't reply, but she could feel a tickle of worry curl in her stomach. Suddenly, she didn't want to be on her own, to go back to an empty house. 'Do you fancy a hot chocolate?'

'You bet! And you can fill me in on whoever stole your heart.'

Connie jabbed him in the ribs. 'Come on.'

They saw Esther safely to her door, and Connie noticed that the girl's excitement faded the closer they got to the Brooks's house. Connie wondered what reception might be awaiting Esther at home. But she dismissed the thought, reminding herself that Esther's mother had given permission, so presumably there wouldn't be too much disapproval.

They waved as Esther opened the door, waving back to them. As they walked on past the house, they saw the glint of light glancing off a pair of binoculars.

'What was that?' Oliver asked, turning his head.

'Our resident Mary Whitehouse. It's Mrs Brooks, Esther's mother, the vicar's wife – I imagine she's making a note of who was at the film. She's probably apoplectic with rage at all the sinful goings on tonight. I was really surprised that she let Esther come.'

'Okay – I'll look forward to meeting this woman. In the meantime, I need hot chocolate. Do you have anything a little bit alcoholic to go with it?'

'I might be able to rustle something up.' Connie looped her arm in his and led the way.

Working in the almost entirely female environment of nursing, and having gone to an all-girls grammar school, Connie's experience of the opposite sex had been limited to patients, her brother and some of her brother's friends, and friends' brothers. Even so, she had gone out with boys at home as it had somehow been expected, but she had not felt a real physical connection with any of them. To keep her mother happy, and in order to have something to gossip about with her friends, Connie had found Charlie, who had been happy to fit the 'boyfriend' role, but who, like her wasn't interested in anything physical. They went out in a desultory fashion, now and then, to films and parties where partners seemed necessary. They had never discussed their relationship, such as it was, and Charlie was equally as content with a goodnight peck on the cheek as Connie. She had been happy to leave it at that. She hadn't even told him that she was leaving, and now felt a twinge of shame, wondering if he had felt any of the hurt she herself had felt at the sudden absence of Daisy. She made a vow to write to him soon – she at least owed him that.

And now, arm in arm with Oliver, to her relief, Connie felt the same as she had with Charlie, that Oliver had no expectation of anything more than a hot drink and a good gossip.

An hour or so later, just as Oliver was going, and feeling relaxed after the best fun she had had in a long time, Connie tensed as the phone rang twice. She waited for a third ring, her heart thumping, the party atmosphere of the evening gone in a moment.

'What's happening? Are you alright, Connie?' Oliver was motionless, one boot on and one socked foot hovering above the other, as he rested his hand on the wall. Before she could answer, there was a frantic banging at the door.

'We need to go now! Koola needs us.' Ilannaq didn't bother with pleasantries.

'What...?' Giving Oliver a hurried wave goodbye, as he put his other boot on, obviously recognising the urgency of the situation, Connie struggled into her own parka and *kamiks* as Ilannaq explained: 'Koola, my sister-in-law she's in labour and the baby won't come. She needs you!'

'We need to get some equipment.' As they flew to the Nurse's Station, Connie made a mental list of everything they would need. They loaded up two skidoos – Connie had learnt that you never went out on one skidoo in the snow in case it broke down. You always took two. The route through the settlement to Koola's house was well-known to Connie, as Ilannaq's brother-in-law, Ishuaktoo, worked at the Hudson Bay, and they managed the journey in record time.

When they reached her, Koola lay pale and exhausted, and Connie could see the desperation etched on the faces of Ilannaq's family. Putting down her bag, she knelt beside Koola and took her hand. 'Don't worry, Koola, it's okay, it's okay.' Although Ilannaq translated, the universal language of emotion surpassed the barrier of spoken language, and Koola gripped her hand as if clinging to a life raft. The Shaman and Koola's grandmother, who often acted as the unofficial midwife for Inuit births in the settlement, were talking to Ilannaq in rapid Inuktitut, and casting doubtful looks at Koola.

Ilannaq turned to Connie. 'The shaman says that the spirits are not happy and they will take this baby's life. Someone in the community has made them angry.'

Connie willing herself to stay calm said to Ilannaq, 'Can you somehow get everyone to leave and give Koola some space – she doesn't need all this right now.' Ilannaq nodded and whatever she said did the trick as Connie and Koola were left alone. Connie could see the gratitude on Koola's eyes, along with the fear.

'Right, let's have a listen to this little one.' She put on an apron and leant over to hear the baby's heartbeat. She could tell immediately that the baby was distressed. Something needed to be done quickly if this little one was going to survive. Busying herself with getting equipment from her bag, Connie frantically cast her mind back to the brief training she'd had in Montreal, and a recent conversation about a breech birth with Patty. In spite of the urgency of the situation, Connie knew that there was a logical process that needed to be followed. First, she needed to do an internal examination, so asking Ilannaq to tell Koola what she was going to do, Connie put on surgical gloves, her heart pounding.

She could tell immediately that the baby was in a breech position, explaining the problem to Ilannaq, who in turn told Koola. Connie could see the growing fear and terror in Koola's eyes, exhausted as she was.

'Tell her that I need to turn the baby around, and then it will be able to come.' Connie spoke with a confidence she didn't feel. She had read about breech births and knew the theory, but now she had to do it for real. There was no time to administer any pain relief. Taking a deep breath and with an authority that seemed to come from nowhere, she explained exactly what she was going to do, and while Ilannaq was telling the onlooking audience that had gradually reappeared in spite of her best efforts, with a firm grip, Connie tried to turn the baby. It seemed wedged into place. Taking a deep breath and willing herself to stay calm and professional, she tried again with more force, and this time the baby shifted into a perfect position, head down.

'Okay,' she said through a sigh of relief. 'Tell Koola to push at the next contraction, tell her to push as hard as she can.'

Ilannaq gripped her sister-in-law's hand as the next contraction came. 'Tell her I can see the baby's head.' Connie had never felt such relief.

'Come on, Koola, you can do this,' she muttered. 'Next contraction, push again, hard.'

When the baby was born there was a tense silence as Connie picked the baby up in a blanket and rubbed him gently, willing him to recover from the shock of the birth. When, at last, he opened his mouth and produced evidence of a healthy pair of lungs, there were cheers and stamping of feet.

Connie cut the cord and handed the little boy to his exhausted mother, who took Connie's hand, tears coursing down her cheeks. 'She says thank you,' translated Ilannaq unnecessarily.

Required to stay for the obligatory tea and celebration, it was early the next morning before Connie got home. Once she had divested herself of all the outer clothing, she sat looking out over the bay in the dim light that now passed as daylight and marvelled at what she had just pulled off. In a hospital situation at home, a newly qualified nurse like Connie would have not been allowed anywhere near a breech birth, such complications generally being the exclusive territory of white-coated consultants. 'Well done, Sanders,' she toasted herself.

As she drifted off to sleep, Connie's elation at her success was replaced by memories of the shaman, whose angry face loomed large. He was not happy that his prediction had been proved wrong. Ilannaq had explained that the shaman would believe that the will of the spirits had been thwarted. Also, there was an uncomfortable element of humiliation and questioning of his authority in the community. But Ilannaq explained that her family were so relieved to have a healthy baby that the shaman's concerns were of secondary importance. People took notice of what her father said. Even so, Connie couldn't get the malevolent hatred in that face out of her dreams, and her sleep was not refreshing.

# Chapter Seventeen

The following morning, as Connie was standing at the window enjoying her first coffee of the day and trying to summon up some energy after only a few hours of sleep, someone burst into the room behind her.

She turned expecting Elizabeth, François, or maybe Oliver, but froze to the spot as she took in the anger evident in Mrs Brooks's face as she strode towards Connie. Grabbing her arm and pinching it hard, she hissed into Connie's face. 'How dare you! I thought you were a bad influence, but I never thought you would corrupt my daughter in such a blatant manner.'

'If this is about the film—' The pieces started to fall into place.

'Yes, it is about the film, corrupting my daughter with this..*filth.*' She could hardly get the word past her anger.

'Esther told me she had your permission. I would never have taken her otherwise.'

'A likely story.' She took a step back. 'My daughter would never tell such a lie.'

'Surely going to see a film can't be that bad a thing. She is twelve and deserves to join in with a bit of fun.' Connie instinctively felt the urge to argue Esther's corner.

Mrs Brooks stared at her with bulbous eyes, and was momentarily rendered speechless.

Connie, in spite of her shock – or maybe because of it – felt a sudden urge to giggle. But, she sternly reminded herself, she was not at school or on the ward now, where authority could be mocked and challenged. She had seriously upset this woman and if her life here was going to be in any way bearable, she had to back down, to take her anger seriously.

'Look, I'm sorry Mrs Brooks. I'm sorry that you feel I've disrespected you, but I honestly thought that you had given permission. I would never have taken Esther otherwise.'

Now, seemingly exhausted by her rage, Mrs Brooks sat heavily on the settee. 'I shall speak to Esther.' She spoke through clenched teeth, but her fire was gone and Connie felt a twinge of sadness for this little woman with such a small life.

'Please don't be too hard on her.'

'I'll thank you to mind your own business with regards to my daughter.' Mrs Brooks tried to summon her previous anger, but Connie could tell she was spent.

After a few seconds, she took a breath and struggled to get up from the settee, angrily pushing Connie's arm aside as she tried to help.

'I don't need your help, thank you, Nurse Sanders,' she said breathlessly.

After Mrs Brooks had gone, Connie wondered what the outcome of all this would be.

It was still as challenging as ever to know the time, as now the everlasting daylight had been replaced by a permanent twilight that seemed to be growing darker by the day. Connie saw Rev and Mrs Brooks emerge through the gloom on her way home after updating her notes and treating some minor ailments at the Nurse's Station, and her heart sank. Had Mrs Brooks brought her husband as back-up for her anger? Connie braced herself for a further onslaught.

'Nurse Sanders! I hear congratulations are in order. You did great work delivering Koola's baby. The family are powerful in their community and hopefully they will feel happier about using your services in the future.' Rev Brooks peered at her.

'Thank you, Rev Brooks.' Connie answered, unsure of where this conversation might lead.

'These people need to understand that mumbo jumbo and occult practices will not save their lives – they are making pacts with the devil.' Connie could detect the familiar hardness and anger in Mrs Brooks's tone, even though she couldn't see her face clearly. It seemed that Elvis was not to be the subject of the conversation, after all. Connie's relief was tempered by another vision of the shaman's face from her nightmares, and she shuddered. Could he have put a curse on her? Did the shaman have real powers? She needed to get a grip – lack of sleep was making her paranoid.

'Oh, Nurse Sanders! The hero of the hour.' Paul Archer had approached, unseen in the gloom. Connie couldn't help detecting a hint of sarcasm in his tone. 'I'm glad you and Esther enjoyed dancing to Elvis the other night.' Connie's heart sank. There was no avoiding Elvis now.

'Thank you, Paul. That will be enough.' Rev Brooks's tone was firm as he steadied his wife who swayed beside him.

Seizing the moment, Connie excused herself and head down, hurried home, determined not to let anyone take away from her pride at the saving of a baby's life...and that of her mother.

A few days later, Koola came to the Nurse's Station, accompanied by Ishuaktoo, to have her baby checked and weighed, signs of the exhausting labour she had endured still evident in the pallor of her face. As Ilannaq proudly showed them everything the newly refurbished Nurse's Station had to offer, Connie realised all over again that this family's connection with the healthcare she was offering was invaluable in getting the Inuit on side. The baby was pronounced fine and healthy, and the couple again expressed their gratitude for what Connie had done. She was moved by the tears in the young father's eyes, and an idea took root in her mind: What if she could run some classes for expectant mothers here at the Nurse's Station? She made a mental note to discuss it with Ilannaq.

Connie's second conversation with her parents was not much of an improvement on the first, as they struggled to get to grips with this unknown person called Roger.

'Is he nice? You seem to mention him a lot, Connie.'

There was a pause as Connie rolled her eyes and looked at the ceiling.

'You might meet a nice young man over there – a Canadian would be exciting.'

'I'm here to work, Mum, not find someone to marry.' Connie immediately regretted the sharpness in her voice and tried to make amends. 'We've got a sort of cinema here now, with a projector and films sent from Frobisher Bay. We watched Elvis Presley the other night.'

She heard her mother sniff disapprovingly. 'I'm not sure about all that jiving about. It doesn't look natural. Why can't they dance properly, like Fred and Ginger?'

Sensing that a different tack was needed if she was to rescue the conversation, Connie changed the subject. 'I delivered a baby a few weeks ago – it was a breech birth. Thank goodness I had a little bit of training in Montreal.'

'Well, I hope they appreciate you.' Her father's voice sounded faint, as if he was struggling to speak. 'We miss you, Cons.'

The use of the childhood pet name almost broke Connie's resolve to stay strong. She swallowed hard. 'I miss you too. But don't worry, I'm absolutely fine and I'll be home before you know it. I need to go now. Give my love to everybody... Roger and out.'

She was just able to make out her mother saying, 'I didn't realise Roger was there...'

Connie pressed the palms of her hands into her eyes and tried to stifle a sob. Fortunately, there was no one else waiting to use the radio and the office was deserted. Thank God! She couldn't have faced Paul...or Jim this time.

Once outside, the darkness seemed even more all-encompassing after the bright strip lights of the Hudson Bay office.

Getting home, she yearned for a pair of thick curtains to shut out the endless white, now shrouded in black. What she would have given for the glow of streetlights and the roar of passing cars and buses. She saw her parents, cosy in front of a coal fire, curtains closed. She even missed the Manchester rain – there was very little rain in the Arctic she had discovered, only snow...and wind. Wind that howled around the settlement like the wolves she sometimes heard in the distance. She even missed the toxic smog and could see her parents' street, the wet pavements glistening in the dim streetlights, their neighbours rushing home early from work as the siren sounded, scarves and handkerchiefs over their mouths and noses. If only she could shut out the Arctic for a few hours. Maybe Pam had had a point about turning her back on the view, after all!

In the absence of a comforting fireside, she got into bed and pulled the covers over her head as the reality hit her that she would not see the sun, or even daylight, for months. The future seemed dark and impenetrable save for the menacing shaman glaring at her with dark eyes that seemed to grow larger and larger. She opened her eyes and headed for the whisky she had stored – desperate for something to give her the oblivion of sleep.

# Chapter Eighteen

C onnie awoke, tangled in her lemon dressing gown, to the smell of strong coffee. Ilannaq smiled and stood up from an awkward crouching position. 'I thought this might bring you around. It's taken a while though – holding the cup under your nose.' She put a hand to the small of her back, feigning pain and groaning.

'Well, I'm awake now, and thank you, Ilannaq.' Connie managed to utter the words as she gingerly sat up, stiff from hours of welcome oblivion on the settee. But now reality was crashing back in with too much force. She put her head in her hands, rocking from side to side. All the old demons, returning unbidden, threatened to overwhelm. She should never have come here.

'We can't give up, there is much to do,' said Ilannaq softly but firmly, her hand around Connie's shoulders. 'You have patients waiting.'

'Waiting? Where?' Connie lifted her head,

'At the Nurse's Station. Word has spread about your healing powers and people need you. I need you.'

Connie met Ilannaq's steady gaze and remembered Elizabeth's warning that homesickness could come from nowhere. She had survived this far, hadn't she? And the unusual sensation of feeling needed, that she was of some importance, galvanised her in to action.

Gulping the coffee down, she asked Ilannaq to prepare some bread with lots of butter while she got herself ready. Relief flooded Ilannaq's face as she leapt into action to prepare Connie's breakfast.

Thirty minutes later they were at the Nurse's Station, where a group of several Inuit were gathered. Connie smiled as the thought came to her that they had not yet learnt the British way of queuing. Would that element of western culture also become the norm at some point? She didn't need to worry about squabbles over who was to be first, however, as Ilannaq briskly took charge and sent in the most serious case first.

Connie had never seen a gunshot wound before and had to steel herself to gently cut away the sleeve of Amaruq's caribou-hide shirt, checking with a gesture to Ilannaq who translated, receiving a nod of assent from Amaruq before she started. She already understood the value of items of clothing for the Inuit and knew that much work would be involved in making a replacement garment of such quality.

Like all Inuit hunters, Amaruq wore an inner layer with the fur facing towards the skin to preserve body heat and creating a barrier with the outer layer which was worn with fur facing outwards. In this case, removing the blood-encrusted sleeve with congealed fur around the wound involved careful and gentle cleaning. Amaruq remained stoic throughout the whole process, hardly flinching. Once she could inspect the wound, Connie saw to her relief that it was only flesh deep. She asked, via Ilannaq, how the accident had happened, knowing that the Inuit were skilled hunters and were unlikely to make mistakes with guns. When she learnt that the gun shot had happened as a result of a drunken brawl, Connie firmly pressed her lips together. This was not the time to launch into a rant about the Western influence on Inuit culture. This was real, and no lamenting the fact would change things. The clock could not be turned back, and maybe Ilannaq was right, her people could not live in isolation from the rest of the world forever. But Connie still mourned inwardly for their loss of a simpler, more innocent life. She was beginning to realise that Daisy had been right – things were not as black and white as she had naïvely assumed – the real world was complex and nuanced. Connie was learning that hasty judgements about things and people was a part of her younger more ignorant self which she was rapidly leaving behind.

She asked Ilannaq to tell Amaruq that she would make the pain go away as she removed the bullet, this time taking care to keep the needle well out of sight. Without being asked, Ilannaq instinctively kept Amaruq talking and distracted him as Connie injected the local anaesthetic into his arm, waiting for it to take effect. After a few anxious minutes, Connie's foray into the same arm with a small pair of sterile forceps resulted in successful location and extraction of the bullet. Without thinking, and flushed with success, she held the offending object aloft and waved it in front of Amaruq's eyes, at which point he promptly passed out.

Once revived, Amaruq was sent on his way with his wound cleaned and stitched and a supply of antibiotics which, in spite of Connie and Ilannaq's warnings, were generally known as magic tablets and a sign of good fortune.

The other patients, who had waited without complaint had minor ailments which needed pain killers and, in one case, antibiotics for a throat infection. Once they had finished and cleaned up, having made meticulous notes in her records, Connie realised that it was the end of the afternoon and the day had passed without the return of homesickness or visions of the shaman's face appearing at all.

She hugged Ilannaq and wondered what she would have ever done without her. 'Thank you, Ilannaq...for today.'

'You seem okay now,' she said patting Connie's back. 'You see, we do need you.'

Connie dashed the tears from her eyes with the back of her hand and could think of nothing else to say except to give Ilannaq another warm hug.

'You should be a nurse – you are a natural, you know just what to do.'

Ilannaq's eyes opened wide. 'You think I could be a nurse? A real one, like you?'

'I do. But whether the Canadian government would agree is another thing.'

As Ilannaq's face fell Connie added, thinking aloud, 'But maybe, if we can get your writing and reading to a good level... How could they refuse?'

As Ilannaq looked at her in wonder, Connie ploughed on; 'I could help you and maybe Rev Brooks could too. After all, he brought you home and recognised your abilities. Let me see what I can do.'

As she was about to leave, another thought came to Connie. 'What do you think about having a little group, here, for pregnant women? We could tell them about labour and how to look after their babies. We have groups like that at home...' Her speech tailed off at the look of bemusement on Ilannaq's face.

'Why?' she shrugged, throwing out her hands.

'Because we could help?' Connie finished, weakly.

'But our mothers don't need help. They have their mothers, aunts and grandmothers. We all know what we are doing and how to raise our babies.' There was a tone of impatience in Ilannaq's voice. 'But if there *is* a problem, now we have you.' She grinned, all irritation gone in a flash.

Connie took a breath. 'Of course, you're right, Ilannaq. I'm sorry. I didn't mean to say that your people don't know how to have babies.' Connie felt a flush rise up through her neck and cheeks. How could she have been so thoughtless and insensitive?

'But the other idea, of me being a nurse? I like that.' Ilannaq threw her head back and laughed. 'Stick with that idea, Connie.'

Later, musing over a welcome cup of hot chocolate, Connie was grateful for a disaster narrowly averted, thanks to Ilannaq. She wondered if she had promised too much, but she was determined to try her best. Ilannaq's community deserved a qualified nurse of their own.

# Chapter Nineteen

The next morning, before her resolve evaporated, Connie headed into the lion's den. A pale and drawn Mrs Brooks answered her knock, and with some reluctance granted her request to see Rev Brooks. She showed Connie to her husband's study with a curt, 'Nurse Sanders to see you.' Closing the door firmly behind her.

The older man looked up and took off his glasses. 'A welcome break, Nurse Sanders. I'm grappling with a particularly tricky passage in St Luke's gospel.'

'The Inuit will be thrilled to have the Bible in their own language,' Connie volunteered, putting aside her misgivings about the conversion of the Inuit to Christianity and all that it entailed.

Rev Brooks nodded in appreciation, and putting down his pen, gave Connie his full attention. 'What can I do for you?'

He listened steadily as Connie outlined her proposal to prepare Ilannaq for application to the nursing school in Montreal. 'Do you think it's a possibility?' she asked finally.

Rev Brooks, looked down at his desk and back at Connie as she held her breath. 'I think it's an excellent idea, and there is no one more able than Ilannaq to get to the stage needed to apply. She is a quick learner. It is going to be important for her community to have their own nurses and other medical staff as time goes on, so this is as good a time to start as any. I think you might be something of a pioneer, Nurse Sanders. Let me make some enquiries and I'll get back to you.'

'Thank you, Reverend Brooks.' As Connie stood, she paused before heading for the door. 'And I am truly sorry about Esther coming to the film. If I had known... I would never have—'

Raising a hand, the clergyman cut her short. 'You don't need to apologise, and I don't think any lasting harm has been done.' There was an unmistakeable twinkle in his eye, and Connie wondered if he had ever seen an Elvis film, and whether he would have been so forgiving if he had.

Rev Brooks sighed heavily, rubbing his hand over his face. 'We cannot keep Esther wrapped up in cotton wool here for ever. She is getting to an age where she needs to be around others of her own age and culture, she will not be a child for much longer and we will have to let her have some freedom. Mrs Brooks will find it hard to let her go I think, so we need to take things slowly.' He gave her a deep, meaningful look.

Connie understood the message: Don't rock the boat, be a bit more understanding, and maybe support my wife as and when she needs it. Connie gave a firm nod back, saying, 'I understand.'

As Connie was making her way past the loud ticking of a grandfather clock on her way to the front door, Mrs Brooks suddenly materialised from the sitting room. Connie felt the heat rising to her cheeks. She had no appetite for further battles with this woman.

'Could you spare a moment, Nurse Sanders?'

Remembering her unspoken agreement with Rev Brooks, Connie repressed an inward sigh. 'Yes, of course, Mrs Brooks.'

As Connie sat on the edge of one of the chintz armchairs – no cocoa this time – her adversary stood before her, making

Connie feel at an uncomfortable disadvantage. She braced herself for the onslaught to come.

'I owe you an apology.'

Ignoring Connie's open mouth, she continued, 'I have spoken with Esther, and she has admitted that she deceived you. I am ashamed and appalled at her lie and she has been confined to her room for two weeks, apart from lessons and a short walk.'

Connie suppressed her outrage at such treatment and kept her tone level, replying, 'I know that it must have upset you greatly, Mrs Brooks, but maybe something...more positive, something to distract Esther from...less corrupting activities might be possible.'

'Such as?'

'I know she is keen to write and that she loves books. Maybe some encouragement in that direction would be good.' An idea was rapidly forming in Connie's mind. Was she over-stepping the mark? But she couldn't let it go, and so taking a firm grip of the edge of the chair, she continued. 'I have been speaking to your husband about the possibility of Ilannaq improving her written and reading skills in order to think about applying to train as a nurse. Do you think Esther – under your supervision of course – would enjoy working with Ilannaq on this?'

Mrs Brooks sank on to the settee, her pallor noticeable in the pale light of a single lamp. 'I would need to discuss this with Rev Brooks of course, but yes, it could give Esther something to focus on,' she said after some thought, looking at the gloom through the window. 'And I could ensure that her learning continued at the same time...' She closed her eyes and sat back against the cushions.

Connie felt a prickle of alarm. 'Are you alright, Mrs Brooks?'

'It will pass, I just get these dizzy spells from time to time. Nothing to worry about.' She forced herself on to her feet.

'I think the stress you're under must be hard to endure...living here with such...different people.'

Connie had hit a raw spot and to her alarm the indomitable Mrs Brooks crumbled before her eyes, falling back on to the settee again. 'Sometimes I just wish we could go home. We have been away for so long. Richard – Rev Brooks says we will retire back to Winchester when his work is finished. I can't wait to have a little house in the cathedral close. He is a canon there, you see.' Her eyes became dreamy. 'I should so love to hear the choir sing Evensong and join the clergy wives' meetings.'

The silence lasted for several minutes, and Connie thought it wise not to break it.

Mrs Brooks clasped her hands and sighed. 'But enough self-indulgence for one day. God has sent us here and we must do his bidding.' She stood, with more purpose this time, and Connie followed suit. 'Rev Brooks and I will talk over your proposal, and...thank you for listening. I know it's not been easy for you either, and I apologise if I've made things harder than they needed to be.'

Connie took her hand warmly. 'We all have to make the best of where we are, but I don't think there is anything wrong with admitting it's hard sometimes.'

As she was in the doorway, Connie turned. 'If those dizzy spells continue, let me know and I can do some tests to see if there is a problem that needs dealing with.'

'I'm sure it's nothing that prayer won't sort out.' Mrs Brooks had recovered her indomitable aura. 'Good day, Nurse Sanders.'

# Chapter Twenty

C onnie couldn't hide her excitement as Daisy emerged from the Twin Otter – able to land safely now that the bay had frozen over. She waved big arcs with her arms as Daisy approached and then enveloped her in a warm hug.

'Wow! Some welcome, Nurse Sanders,' Daisy said taking a quick step back and picking up some of the luggage that had come with her.

Connie's heart stopped. Had she overdone it?

'It's good to see you too, Connie.' Connie relaxed at the warm smile.

'Let me help you with some of these. Bring your stuff to mine – it's nearer. We can take things to yours on the skidoos from there.' They trudged toward the settlement, Connie finding the cold air fizzing in her lungs exhilarating.

Once everything was inside, they sat together with hot drinks laced with whisky looking at the dim twilight.

'I'm thinking of turning the settee sideways a bit so that I don't have to look at this permanent darkness all the time. In fact, I'd rather face the lamp!'

Daisy gave a sudden hearty laugh. 'Why, Nurse Sanders, I seem to remember you saying only a few months ago that you couldn't understand why anyone would want to turn their back on this view! And as I recall, you were very disparaging about predecessor's room layout. Poor Pam!'

Connie kicked Daisy's foot playfully. 'I know, I know. But I've learnt that there is only so much ice and snow, and darkness, I can cope with at the end of a long day. Sometimes I just need to look at a warm glow.'

'Maybe we could get a mural of a log fire...' Daisy left the sentence hanging, a thoughtful expression on her face.

Thinking that she was teasing, Connie turned to give her a playful punch, but froze.

'You're actually serious, aren't you?'

'Leave it with me...'

Connie groaned, 'What? No! That's ridiculous.' She got up to refill their mugs, hastily changing the subject. 'What news about the carvings?'

'Good news, actually. There is definitely a market and some other Inuit communities are already forming cooperatives to sell their pieces. We need to get Moosasee, Hanta, and the other settlement elders together to see if they would like to follow suit. I met a dealer in Montreal who has a gallery where the pieces can be sold.'

'That's amazing, Daisy. I'm sure they'll be thrilled!' Connie clapped her hands.

'Also, Peter – the dealer – thought it would be a good idea to have pictures of the Inuit at work on the carvings. It would provide extra interest and a level of provenance.'

'I could do that. I already have some photos that I've taken around the settlement.' Connie felt the excitement building. Some of my first prints have come back so I've already got some that are good enough. And I'm learning to adjust the lighting and exposure.'

There was silence for a few minutes as they sipped their drinks.

'And...' Connie jumped up, as the thought came to her, almost causing Daisy to spill her drink. 'We could get each carver to have some kind of identifying mark on each of their own pieces.'

'You've really got the bit between your teeth!' Daisy laughed, holding her mug aloft to prevent any spillage. 'And you're right.' She turned to face Connie, placing her mug on the relative safety of the coffee table. 'I was thinking, we need to organise a meeting in the hall. I'll ask Rev Brooks for a time—'

'No, I can do that.' Connie jumped in before she could stop herself. 'Rev Brooks and I have something of a rapport.'

Daisy raised her eyebrows. 'Really?'

When Connie had filled her in on the plans for Ilannaq and the drama of the now infamous Elvis film, Daisy looked at her steadily.

'I turn my back for a few minutes and you've turned from an opinionated youngster to something resembling an adult, Connie.'

Connie blushed at the use of her first name and the unexpected praise. 'Maybe I'm beginning to listen and learn before opening my mouth and making sweeping judgements.'

This time it was Daisy who enveloped Connie in a warm hug, and Connie felt her heart sing.

Connie found Rev Brooks behind his desk as usual, hunched over, straining his eyes to read the documents in front of him.

'I shall be so glad when my new spectacles come, and I can really get back to working at full speed.' He looked up, adjusting his focus. 'Good morning, Nurse Sanders. I have news.'

Connie sat on the chair opposite and waited as Rev Brooks shuffled through his papers.

'Ah here we are. The health authority in Montreal is quite happy to enrol Ilannaq on their nursing training course providing her English is up to scratch. So we have a job to do. They are also pleased that she is working with you, and so will already have acquired some nursing knowledge,' he added.

'Wow, that's wonderful!' Connie once again clapped her hands in joy. Twice within twenty-four hours. What was happening?

'I've heard about your suggestion of including Esther in this project.' He looked at her with a steady gaze and Connie felt a twinge of discomfort in her stomach. Had she blown it all with her big mouth after trying so hard? 'I think it's a wonderful idea.' He smiled and sat back.

Connie let out a deep breath. 'Oh, I'm so glad.'

'Mrs Brooks will sort everything out and Kathy and Tom are happy to supply some materials from the school. If you can ask Ilannaq what times would be appropriate, we can get started.'

'Thank you so much, Rev Brooks. Ilannaq will be thrilled. Actually, I need to ask you about something else.'

'*Another* scheme?'

Once Connie had filled him in on the details of the planned cooperative, Rev Brooks readily agreed for the hall to be used and gave his backing to the project. 'We need to stop the exploitation of these artists by unscrupulous Westerners – mentioning no names.' Was that a tic, or had Rev Brooks actually winked at her? 'Just let me know when you have a date and time, and the hall is all yours. I had always intended it to serve the community in more ways than just as a school.'

As she was making her way past the grandfather clock, once more, the sitting room door opened, but this time it was Esther, not her mother, who appeared, flushed with excitement, her hair tucked behind her ears.

'Thank you so much, Connie. I can't wait to work with Ilannaq.' There was a pause, and a small frown appeared between her dark brows. 'You don't think she'll mind working with me, do you? Will she think I'm too young? I wouldn't want her to feel insulted.'

'I haven't spoken to her yet, but I'm ninety-nine percent sure she'll be thrilled to bits. She likes you, and if you can help her to become a nurse, well, Bingo!'

Esther laughed. And Connie saw something of the amazing young woman she could become. As she turned to go, Esther touched her arm. 'Connie, I'm so sorry about getting you into trouble about the film. I just didn't think. I just wanted to go so much. But I know it was wrong. Sometimes I just feel...I don't know...I just want to be free – of all this.'

'It's okay, Esther,' Connie soothed the younger girl. 'It's in the past, so let's leave it where it belongs.' Connie patted her hand.

'I did so love the dancing though. I wish I could dance like François. I would love to learn. And...' she lowered her voice, 'Can you keep a secret?' Without waiting for a response, Esther continued, 'I've found a little hiding place where no one can find me. I tell my mother that I'm with Ilannaq but sometimes I just head off to a little cave near Cooper's Pond where I light a fire and just sit and write. Each time I go, I take some wood – there's usually plenty of bits and pieces lying around the Hudson Bay yard. When it's burnt, I come home. It's like my own little space.' Esther looked at Connie with a tinge of anxiety. 'You won't tell...anyone, will you?'

Connie couldn't help thinking that Virginia Woolf would have understood Esther's predicament when she wrote *A Room of One's Own*. Maybe Esther would get to read it one day.

'Do you think I'm bad for doing that?'

Esther's question brought her back to the moment and Connie was unsure of the ethics of this situation, but remembering herself at thirteen replied with a grin, 'Everyone needs a secret or two.' But then she remembered that she was a responsible adult and added, 'But you must never go there when the weather is bad. And you need to tell somebody – maybe Ilannaq as she's your alibi? She would understand, and I'm sure you can trust her. Let me have a word, first. It would only be good manners to ask her.' Connie added, tilting her head to one side. 'Yes?'

'I guess...'

'Good. And in return I'll see what we can do about dancing. But one step at a time. I'll speak to François, and it will have to be cleared by your mother,' Connie said firmly.

Esther's eyes dropped to the floor, the curtain of hair falling forward. 'I know.'

# Chapter Twenty-One

I lannaq did a little dance, Inuit style, hopping from one foot to the other when Connie delivered the good news. 'Thank you, Connie. I can't believe it!'

'Esther is worried that you would feel humiliated by having such a young teacher, even though her mother will be supervising the content of the lessons.'

'I feel sorry for that girl locked away from others of the same age and culture as her own. I know how she feels and I would do anything to give her more confidence.'

Connie closed the record book she was updating. 'I think she will get as much out of it as you. And I know that she will be in safe hands...and that you will respect the Brooks's beliefs and views. Unlike me, who charges in like a bull in a china shop.'

At the look of confusion on Ilannaq's face, Connie laughed. 'It means going in, being clumsy and knocking everything over.'

Ilannaq nodded in understanding. And with a cheeky grin she said, 'I can't comment. But I will remember the bull and the china shop.'

Before Connie could raise the question of Esther's secret, Amaruq appeared in the doorway.

'Is everything all right, Amaruq? Is there a problem with the wound?' Connie took a step towards him. She could hear the barking of dogs nearby.

He spoke in rapid Inuktitut, looking at Connie all the while, and she felt the now familiar frustration at still only being able to understand a smattering of words in his language.

'His father is ill. He thinks he has been not well for some time but did not want to come for help. Since he has seen how you made his son better, he has agreed to see you,' Ilannaq delivered in a calm voice. 'But he is now too ill to get here,' she added.

'Where do they live?' Connie threw over her shoulder, already getting the essentials together that she would need.

'In the second settlement we visited, and had the feast, remember?' Connie gave Ilannaq a stern look, willing her not to mention eyes.

Apparently resisting the temptation, Ilannaq returned to the more important matter at hand. 'Amaruq has brought his dog team to take us. There is a storm brewing and it's not safe on skidoos.' And right on cue a powerful gust of wind blew the door open, depositing a scattering of snow on the floor.

Feeling a strange mixture of excitement at travelling behind a dog team, and terror about what she was going to face at the end of the journey, Connie gave her equipment to Amaruq to stow safely on the sled behind them that acted as a kind of trailer. He called to his dogs and they jumped to attention, ready for his command to move.

They slid through the surreal, grey landscape, buffeted by the wind which was increasing in pace as horizontal arrows of snow and ice battered them from behind. Connie thought about the advert she had answered in what seemed like another age: *Wanted, a nurse with a sense of adventure.* If this wasn't an adventure, she didn't know what was. 'Am I an explorer and adventurer now, Grandad?' She saw his approving smile in her mind's eye as she clung on to Ilannaq for support and warmth, marvelling at how the dogs could run at such speed when visibility was so limited, how they seemed to have a sixth sense about any obstacles or unsafe surfaces, avoiding them with very little instruction from Amaruq. She understood now, how unique and precious the relationship was between a hunter and his dogs, the mutual understanding that they needed each other, even in death. There was no other way they could have made this journey.

All romantic thoughts of adventure disappeared, however, when she saw the state of her first seriously ill patient. Amaruq's father, who couldn't have been more than fifty, had the cavernous, sunken look of an eighty-year-old. She didn't need to examine him to know that he wasn't long for this world if she couldn't get him to a hospital, and could only imagine the pain he must be in. From her examination, she guessed some kind of liver disease was the cause, but she didn't have the equipment or know-how to make an accurate diagnosis.

Turning to Ilannaq, she said, 'We need to get him flown out of here to Frobisher Bay immediately. He is very ill.'

As Ilannaq relayed this to the family, they became agitated, and Connie could see the terror in the eyes of her patient all too clearly. This was the moment she had been dreading, and now it was here, and she had to confront the fact that these proud people were distrustful and frightened of her people – with good reason as far as she could see. Nevertheless, training and instinct kicked in and she repeated her message with more urgency. 'He will die if we don't get him to Frobisher Bay within the next twenty-four hours.'

Ilannaq, calm as ever, took Connie to one side. 'There is no flying in this weather, Connie. And we don't know how long the storm will last.'

Connie felt a stab of panic pass through her body. She was useless. What could she do?

As if reading her thoughts, Ilannaq said, 'Can you make him comfortable and take his pain away? Make his end better?'

Everything in Connie rebelled against giving in and accepting that this man would die under her care. She glanced over at the family and her heart contracted at their evident distress at the suffering of their father. Taking a deep breath and squaring her shoulders, she said, 'You're right, Ilannaq. Yes, I'll give him some morphine to ease the pain and we'll stay and make him comfortable.'

The family were visibly relieved at the news that their father could not be taken from them and that he would have some magic to make the pain go away.

As she prepared the morphine injection, Connie felt eyes on her. She looked up to meet the hostile and slightly triumphant gaze of the shaman, and it took all her willpower to stop the shaking in her hands as she administered the dose. Having done what she could, she and Ilannaq retired to the fireside to allow the family some precious time with their father and grandfather.

She heard the wind howling and whistling outside, a demented monster deprived of its prey, and was thankful for the sturdy protection of the hut. The cleverly constructed dwelling did not flinch under the onslaught, firmly surrounded as it was by tightly packed snow with only one entrance at the front.

Having finished the inevitable cup of strong black tea and eaten some dried fish kindly offered by Amaruq's wife, Connie became aware that Ilannaq was being especially talkative, telling her about the frequency and strength of winter storms, seemingly saying anything that came into her head. Connie's antenna sensed that something was not right, and this sense of unease grew as Amaruq's family returned to the fire in silence, the shaman clearly carrying out some kind of ritual. Ilannaq stopped talking and bowed her head. Then Amaruq's father appeared, walking slowly and unsteadily, but walking, nevertheless.

Connie instinctively cried out and tried to jump up, but as she did so, she felt a firm hand grip her arm and drag her back down to the ground. She hadn't realised that Ilannaq was so strong. There was silence as he slowly made his way out into storm, pierced only by Connie's cry.

'No! No! What are you doing? Come back!' She struggled against Ilannaq's grip as she felt another, more powerful restraining hand on her other arm. Powerless to move, Connie looked wildly around at the motionless family. 'Ilannaq! What are they doing? Stop him!'

'Ilannaq!'

Ilannaq eventually met her gaze and shook her head in a small movement.

'Leave it, Connie,' she said in a low voice.

Connie closed her eyes, wondering if she was trapped in some kind of hideous nightmare. This couldn't be happening!

Eventually the iron grip on her left arm was released, and Connie rushed to the doorway, glimpsing the shimmering form of her patient disappearing into white oblivion, intermittently hidden by gusts of snow – headed to somewhere she knew she could not follow.

Blinded by tears, she was powerless.

Ilannaq appeared at her side. 'It is our way, Connie. It is for the best. He will return to the earth – it is the cycle of life and death. It is bigger than us.'

Connie sniffed and wiped away her tears, willing herself to be calm.

'My people believe that the spirits of our ancestors have called him,' Ilannaq continued calmly. She turned to the family now gathered around their mother. One of the daughters nodded to Connie and spoke.

'She says to thank you for taking her father's pain away so he could perform his final task.'

Connie nodded in return, impressed by the dignity and the calm acceptance of these people of the world they had lived in for centuries. Who was she, Connie Sanders to interfere in this age-old ritual? But everything she had been taught told her this was not right. Unable to resolve her conflicted thoughts and feelings, Connie packed her things away. As she did so she raised her eyes to meet those of the shaman, who gave her a look she could not interpret. Some mixture of triumph but maybe with a tinge of respect? He too nodded before moving back to the family group where he started to perform what Connie guessed might be the equivalent of a funeral service back home.

As they returned, Connie focused on the post-storm silence only broken by the sound of the dogs' harnesses rattling as they moved through the snow, responding to an occasional call from Amaruq. Ilannaq seemed equally lost in her own thoughts and they travelled in the mutually supportive silence of colleagues who have seen death.

From the porch, Connie sensed a presence in her house before she had even reached the front door. She hesitated, exhausted, wanting nothing more than the warm comfort of her bed. Listening closely, all she could hear was some shuffling and a smothered giggle. Not in the mood for flippancy, Connie huffed and threw open the door in annoyance.

Daisy, François, Kathy and Oliver, cheered and clapped, standing side-by-side concealing something behind them. In spite of her exhaustion and sadness, Connie couldn't help smiling and feeling a strange warmth at the sight of her friends gathered in her house.

'Okay. What is it?' She asked, laughing.

They stood aside, François and Daisy going one way, and Oliver and Kathy the other, like the parting of curtains before a performance. Connie gasped at what she saw. There was a log fire complete with mantlepiece and a vase of flowers, painted in vivid, warm, reds, oranges, and yellows. Her hand flew to her mouth. 'What the...?'

'It was Daisy's idea,' said Kathy. She roped us all in, and when we knew you'd been called away, this was our chance.

Connie collapsed onto the settee, now turned away from the window, speechless. Her friends had done this for her? Nothing like this had ever happened to her before. She'd never had friends like this.

'Oliver is a talented artist, apparently,' Daisy said, giving him a playful nudge. The resemblance Connie had felt between him and David became even stronger.

'Wow! Thank you all so much. I love it!'

'Thank goodness for that. We were worried that you might hate it.' Daisy stepped forward and sat beside her on the settee. 'And that would have been very awkward.'

'How did you...?'

'Kathy got a large piece of canvas from the Hudson Bay store and Thierry made a frame for it, and *voila*!' François said, her eyes sparkling.

'Everyone had a go at a few flames, it wasn't just me.' Oliver added with mock modesty.

Connie could feel the heat of the colours brightening the gloom, but most of all she basked in the warmth and love of the friends who had done this for her.

'Thank you so much. What can I say? You are the best friends ever. I've never...' Connie felt the tears running down her cheeks before she was aware that she was crying.

'We know you've had a difficult day,' Oliver sat on her other side, speaking gently. 'But maybe this will help you feel a little bit better. We all care about you, you know.'

'Stop right there, Oliver, unless you want me to become a snivelling wreck,' Connie said holding up her hand, and looking around at the group. 'But thank you.'

Once the others had gone, Connie sat with Daisy, basking in the warmth of the fire.

Talking the events over, Connie came to understand something of the practicalities of death in the unforgiving Arctic.

'Even in the summer when there is no snow, the ground is frozen permafrost. We can't dig a grave – it would be too difficult. The Inuit way of dying is often to walk away until either the cold or a wild animal takes their life.'

Connie shuddered. She understood the reason but found it hard to accept the reality of what she had seen. She remembered how their old cat, Tiddles had hidden under the shed to die when she had been ten, and the tears she had cried at the time. Maybe the animals had the right idea, after all. She needed to let go of childish sentiments if she was to survive in this world.

'Connie, are you listening? You seem miles away.'

'Sorry, Daisy. I think I was just growing up a bit, that's all'

Daisy looked at her with smile that melted Connie's whole being, turning her legs to jelly.

'So, what were you saying?'

'That the Inuit sometimes take loved ones out into the wilderness when they have died and build cairns of stones over them. They will still be eaten eventually by wild animals, so nothing about death is permanent here.'

Connie, feeling spent, with the emotional highs and lows of the day, had nothing to say and leant back on the settee and closed her eyes.

Daisy, seemingly sensing her need for some time alone, and got to her feet, saying. 'Don't forget the meeting in the hall tomorrow evening. I'll see you there.'

And then she was gone.

# Chapter Twenty-Two

The meeting was about to start and there was a sense of expectation in the air that something new and different was about to happen. While they waited for stragglers, the Inuit who had been on time shamelessly and rapidly devoured all the biscuits that had been laid out. Daisy laughed at Connie's open-mouthed amazement. 'These people have had to seize any opportunity to eat for generations and they are hard-wired to eat every morsel that is put in front of them. In fact, they would see it as a discourtesy to their hosts – me and you – if they didn't. Try and summon up a look of appreciation and you'll go far.'

Connie smiled and nodded, hoping she had conveyed the appropriate response.

Eventually, once everyone had arrived, and many were on a sugar high, being unused to Western sugary food, the meeting got under way. Daisy gave the assembled elders and carvers an update on her fact-finding mission. As there were nods of approval from around the room and some questions, Connie once again felt at a disadvantage being not able to join in. She had learnt quite a bit of common, everyday Inuktitut from Ilannaq, but this level of conversation was way out of her league.

Daisy filled her in. 'They are happy to work together to sell their carvings at the price that has been offered, but they are worried that the Hudson Bay won't be happy if they sell their carvings without going through them.'

'You mean give them away through them!' Connie muttered.

'I'm trying to persuade them that they are not bound to sell all their goods through the Bay, but I can see that it's a step into the unknown for them.'

'Well then, we need to be talking to Paul Archer and tell him in advance what the plan is. Prepare the way for a trial run, maybe.' Even as she said it, Connie's stomach churned at the very thought of such a conversation.

Daisy nodded and relayed the suggestion. Moosasee, the most senior of the elders stood and addressed the group. Connie managed to make out a few words, including 'Paul Archer' and sensed a tone of defiance in his voice.

'He says we'll start with a small batch of carving from his own settlement to see what happens. But he says that they only sell furs to the Bay and that carvings are something different and that it's none of Paul Archer's business. After all, he and many of his men have been given carvings for free over the years and have never suggested paying for them, so how could they trust that they would get a fair price?'

There were nods of agreement from some, including Hanta, and uncomfortable silence from others. He spoke again this time with an air of authority.

Daisy translated. 'He is happy with the price we can get and will work out a cooperative system for the first shipment so that all the carvers are paid fairly. He says he will take the risk of the first step with pieces from his own settlement, and the other elders can watch and see what happens. He will also ensure that each carver signs every piece with a distinctive signature. For some of them that will be their disc number as that's how they think they are known on the mainland,' Daisy added ruefully.

There was a ripple of discomfort around the room as Moosasee added something else.

'He is instructing the carvers in his community to stop giving any further pieces to Bay employees.'

Connie observed that, although there was some tension no one dared to defy Moosasee's authority and that cultural allegiances prevailed.

Daisy stood and delivered one more speech, looking at Connie as she spoke – and whatever she said was greeted with smiles and nods. 'They like the idea of you taking photos of the carvers to go with their pieces. They trust you, Connie. You should be proud.'

Connie stood and gave a nod accompanied by an awkward bow, unsure of the protocol for such an occasion.

At the post-meeting debriefing over coffee, Connie and Daisy debated the Hudson Bay issue.

'Paul Archer is not going to be happy about this. I think he and his men have made a tidy sum over the years by exploiting Inuit generosity.' Daisy sighed as she leant back against the cushions. 'I see trouble ahead.'

'This had to happen, we couldn't let things continue as they are, and I know that if it comes to it, Rev Brooks will support us.'

'He will? You've spoken to him about the cooperative?'

'Floated the suggestion, yes. I had to tell him why we needed to use the hall. He doesn't approve of the greed amongst the Bay employees.'

'Goodness, you're well in there, Nurse Sanders. I haven't had as much as a nod from him for months.'

'It's my natural charm...and persuasive skills.' Connie batted Daisy's arm with the back of her hand. 'Talking of the infamous Paul Archer, what *is* his story. I've heard vague rumours around Harbour Inlet about some woman in the past...'

'Well...' Daisy put down her mug and settled herself against the cushions, feet resting on Connie's lap. Connie willed herself not to flinch or push Daisy away. Daisy was not Helen, she reminded herself, and anyway, this was what friends did, wasn't it?

'He used to be a senior officer in the RCMP in Vancouver but fell in love with his superior's wife.'

'What? Paul Archer has emotions other than anger? Ooh I love a good gossip!' Connie wriggled in excitement.

'Sooo, they had an affair, and apparently were planning to run away together.'

'So romantic, I love it!'

'Are you going to let me finish or not?'

'Sorry, sorry. Go on.' Connie motioned zipping her lips closed.

'Well, anyway, his boss came home early one day and found them in bed together. And the proverbial shit hit the fan. The story goes that said boss framed Paul and he was subsequently arrested for evidence tampering and colluding with the local criminal syndicate.'

Connie keeping her lips firmly closed, motioned Daisy to continue.

'The wife, took fright and returned to her husband, accusing Paul of seducing her. So, he took a vow to hate all women forever and ended up here, like the rest of us – all running from some catastrophe or another and vowing to never let it happen again.'

Connie bowed her head and bit her lip willing the blush to disappear, all awareness of Daisy's feet in her lap forgotten.

'A-ha!' Daisy pounced. 'That tell-tale blush says everything, Nurse Sanders.'

Connie couldn't bring herself to speak.

In a gentler voice, moving her legs and taking Connie's hand, she said, 'Are you ready to tell me why you're really here?'

After a silence as she mustered up the courage to tell her equally humiliating sorry story, Connie told Daisy everything about Helen. From the first thrilled excitement of being the centre of her attention, the romantic poetry, the films, and the music they had shared, right up to the devastating announcement of her marriage, delivered in a cold, uncaring statement, as if what they had shared had never happened.

Daisy squeezed Connie's hand and sighed heavily with a shaky breath. 'Oh Connie, I'm so sorry.'

'I feel such an idiot, thinking that she really cared about me! I fell for everything, hook, line and sinker.'

'She is a bitch!' Daisy snarled between clenched teeth. 'How dare she abuse her position in such a way!'

And then the tears came, and Connie sobbed as she had never sobbed before as Daisy held her close.

# Chapter
# Twenty-Three

C onnie awoke with a start, memories of Helen and the emotion of the previous evening still raw. She had relived the moment of Helen's departure in her dreams, followed by an invitation to be one her bridesmaids, and the forced attendance at her wedding. In her dream, Connie had broken ranks from the other bridesmaids at the church to run and shake Helen's shoulder, crying and haranguing her in front of the altar and her family. Somehow, this act of confronting Helen, and exposing her treachery at her own wedding, even if it had only been in a dream, had lanced the abscess of anger, humiliation, hate and fear that had threatened to poison her mind. She became aware of Daisy, still asleep and lying fully clothed on the bed beside her and felt a strange sense of calm.

The moment was rudely interrupted by a single ring shrilling from the phone at urgent intervals. Before she had time to process what any of it meant, she jumped out of bed and picked up the phone.

'Nurse Sanders? Paul Archer here.' Connie heard the inevitable clicks as various other listeners-in around Harbour

Inlet picked up their receivers, as they always did when there was an RCMP call.

'Yes.'

'Is Daisy Scott with you? We have an urgent call for her.'

Before her brain was in gear, Connie replied. 'Yes, she's here. I'll get her.' She rushed over to Daisy, who was sitting up, her wild blonde curls in a tangled mass. 'Daisy, you need to come. Paul Archer's on the phone with an urgent call for you.'

Daisy leapt off the bed and crossed the floor in three long strides. 'Yes? What is it, Paul?'

Connie studied Daisy's face and knew that this could only be bad news. As Daisy replaced the receiver, her pale face was laced with shock. Connie sat her on the settee, feeling her shivering through the thick clothes. 'It's my mother. She has cancer. I need to get to her. They're sending a flight over today or tomorrow, so I need to be on it.'

'Oh Daisy, I'm so sorry. What can I do?'

Daisy sat motionless without answering for a few minutes, so unlike her usual, energetic and purposeful self. Taking her hand, and stoking it, Connie tried to bring her back from wherever she had gone to. 'Daisy?'

'First things first, you can get me a coffee.' In an instant, the usual Daisy was back, and Connie, thankful, sprang into action.

After the second cup of coffee and the inevitable toast, Daisy had fully recovered herself. 'Connie, get to Moosasee and see if they have some carvings that they can get together for me to take to Montreal – fortunately it's where my mother lives, so I'll take them to the gallery while I'm there.'

She looked at Connie and stroked her face, tucking a strand of short hair behind her ear, from where it escaped and promptly fell forward again. Connie willed her to tuck it back again, revelling in the genuine affection behind the gesture. 'I'm sorry, Connie...about all this. Are you okay this morning? I couldn't leave you on your own last night. I just felt that you needed company.'

Connie nodded. 'I'm fine, honestly.' And she was. Talking about Helen had somehow lightened the burden of grief and anger that had weighed her down and had maybe triggered her strangely cathartic dream. She couldn't explain it, and this wasn't the time. Right now, Daisy needed some practical support. 'I did need company...you. And thank you Daisy. But don't worry about me, you need to get ready for the flight.'

And then she was gone, leaving silence behind her, as Connie tried to understand how she felt about Daisy's presence in – or rather *on* – her bed that morning.

The next few days passed in a blur as preparations were made for Daisy's hurried departure. When the Otter took off, taking Daisy and ten Inuit carvings with it, Connie could not hold back the tears, triggered by the maelstrom of emotions churning around in her head. She wondered when she would ever see Daisy again. She had taken a big step in trusting Daisy with her feelings and had been surprised and warmed by Daisy's unquestioning support. And now, Daisy had been taken away from her. Was this to be the pattern of Connie's life? Building trust with someone who then disappeared? Feeling ashamed of the self-pity threatening to overwhelm her, Connie reminded herself sternly that none of this was Daisy's fault. In fact, she would have been horrified if Daisy had not gone. She knew that Daisy's relationship with her mother had been fraught, but she had not hesitated to go to her side when she needed help. Connie took comfort from that. François came over and put an arm around Connie's shoulders. 'Do not worry, *ma chérie*, she will be back.' She turned Connie to face her and wiped away a stray tear with her thumb. 'In the meantime, we have dancing classes to organise!'

'We do?'

'Yes. Mrs Brooks has said that Esther can learn to dance! I told her a growing girl needs more exercise than she is currently getting, and to think of it as – how do you say? – P.E.? at school.'

'François, you are amazing!' Connie hugged her. 'When are we starting?'

'I'm meeting Esther this afternoon – she is coming to my 'ouse. I thought we would start with the jive.' François gave a mischievous grin.

'I love it!'

They started with the basic jive steps, accompanied by François's battery powered record player – of which Connie was extremely envious, moving onto kicks and flicks. The sight of Esther having fun, warmed Connie's heart and banished all the sadness and confusion of earlier – at least for a few hours. For now, she was having fun.

When the music stopped, they were aware of knocking and someone appeared in the doorway. Connie did her best to conceal her surprise as Paul Archer stepped into the room. 'I hear there are dancing classes going on, and wondered if I might join in.'

If François was as astonished as Connie, she hid it well, holding out her hand to take Paul's dragging him into the centre of the room. 'How about we give a little jive demonstration for our pupils?'

'Of course.'

Connie reflected that as Thierry was friends with Paul, François's relationship with him might be less fraught than her own.

There was no doubting that François and Paul knew how to jive, and Connie and Esther watched with rapt attention as they kicked, flicked, swirled, and Paul lifted François off the ground in a thrilling final flourish.

Connie and Esther clapped enthusiastically as François and Paul gave an out-of-breath bow.

'I'm pretty out of condition these days,' said Paul ruefully.

'Not like in your competition days,' observed François archly.

'You danced in competitions?' Esther gasped, eyes wide.

'You are looking at the Canadian Latin and jive champion for two years running.' François saluted Paul with a flourish of her arms.

As Esther and Connie gasped, Paul responded, 'It was a long time ago now, François.'

'We used to meet at lots of competitions, but no one could beat Paul.' François winked at him.

Connie was beginning to see that there was more to Paul than she had thought, and a little seed of empathy for what he had been through started to germinate in her heart.

Her softening of attitude towards him was short lived though, as when he met her the following day at the Hudson Bay offices, the old Paul had returned with a vengeance.

'How dare you interfere in things that are nothing to do with you!' Connie braced herself for the onslaught. She knew what this was about but had not reckoned on dealing with the fall-out about the carvings without Daisy's support.

Taking a deep breath and channelling her inner Daisy, she closed the door of the office. 'Let's talk about this without shouting, shall we?' She indicated for him to sit down, while she perched on the edge of his desk. Connie had learnt a few lessons about height giving you superiority in a confrontation from Paul himself. But this time, taken aback by her command of the situation, he had fallen into his own trap and was now unable to move without acknowledging it.

'Firstly, the Hudson Bay does not have a monopoly over Inuit trading, and certainly not where works of art are concerned.' Connie was amazed at the calm authoritative voice that came out of her mouth. 'And secondly, you have no right to sell Inuit carvings without sharing the proceeds with the artists who created them.'

Paul changed tactics, affecting a nonchalant attitude, as he leant back in his chair, crossing one leg over the other. 'What does it matter? If they choose to give these…home-made carvings away, they're ours to dispose of as we see fit.'

'You know their true worth as well as I do, and now, thanks to Daisy, so do the Inuit.'

'Thanks to you and your…*girlfriend* interfering!' he spat out.

Connie froze. '*What?*'

'Oh yes, that hit home, didn't it? Don't think I don't know what's going on between you two – her staying over at your house. *I* know, even if everyone else hasn't put two and two together…*yet.*'

He leant back in the chair, a smug grin on his face at the veiled threat.

Connie was determined not to let Paul see the physical evidence of the fury raging in her heart. Instead, she stood slowly looking him in the eye and turned to open the door. 'I don't think we have anything else to discuss here.' She made the coldness in her tone into icy arrows.

By the time she arrived back at the Nurse's Station, the shaking had stopped, and Connie was aware of a calm anger and strength that she had never felt before. Gone was the angry, vulnerable teenager, constantly pushing against authority and who was quick to judge, and instead a rational, cool-headed adult was emerging, who could think strategically and who was not going to be intimidated by the likes of Paul Archer. Especially where the exploitation of her friends was concerned. And she realised that, yes, many of these brave and proud Inuit were her friends now, and she felt proud that they had accepted her.

# Chapter
# Twenty-Four

A s Christmas approached, Ilannaq was proud to demon-
strate her newly acquired reading and writing skills to
Connie. 'Esther and me? We are like this.' She linked two of
her fingers together and held them up to show Connie. 'She
is a good teacher.'

'And you are a good friend for her to have,' Connie returne.
She was thrilled at the new, more confident Esther that was
beginning to emerge. Teaching and dancing had given her a
sparkle and sense of fun that Connie had never known existed
behind the curtain of hair, which these days was tied back in
a high ponytail, curtesy of François, who had justified it to
Mrs Brooks as Esther's 'P.E. hair'. Esther had also confided in
her that she was trying to write something each day, to record
her life in this remote community. Connie wondered if she
realised how truly unique her story would be.

Wondering at the lack of patients not-queuing outside
the Nurse's Station, Connie spent the morning updating her
scrupulous records, of which she was inordinately proud.
When she commented on how quiet things were to Ilannaq,

her companion shuffled her feet in an uncharacteristically uncomfortable way as Connie gave her a quizzical look.

'It's just one of those days today,' she said with a forced smile. Connie shrugged not entirely reassured but nevertheless headed over to François's, looking forward to an afternoon of dancing. They were about to embark on the American Smooth, Fred and Ginger style. Connie loved the romance of these films and couldn't wait to start learning something she could maybe impress Daisy with, on her return. And the group was growing with the recent addition of Oliver and Kathy.

She had received a few letters from Daisy, and it seemed that her mother was needing around the clock care. She sensed a tiredness in Daisy's writing in the second letter, and, concerned, wondered how long she would be able to keep going on her own with no help. There was some good news though – all of the carvings that she had taken to the gallery had sold, and the gallery was arranging payment to Moosasee via the Hudson Bay. Connie had told Daisy all about her encounter with Paul and reassured her that Rev Brooks would personally oversee the payment process. Connie did not mention, however, the sleazy, veiled threat Paul had made at the end of their confrontation. Daisy didn't need to hear that. If Paul was going to be there today, she would brazen it out and act as if nothing had happened. She was pretty sure he wouldn't make sly comments in front of this particular group of people.

She was just taking off her hat and parka when François appeared. She looked uncomfortable.

'What is it, François?'

'I'm so sorry, Connie.' She looked at the floor unable to meet her eyes.

Connie felt a familiar prickle of fear. 'What is it?' she asked sensing bad news.

'Mrs Brooks has said that the dancing lessons cannot continue if you are present.'

'What? Why?'

François sniffed back a sob. 'She says you are a bad person to be around Esther.'

Connie stared at François, who looked away, unable to conceal her embarrassment.

'Okay, I understand. I'll go.' She said quickly, once she had recovered from the shock, and wanting to spare François. 'But this is not your fault, François, she added firmly. I'll go and speak to Mrs Brooks myself and find out what's going on.'

On her way out, she met Paul. 'Sorry to hear that you're not welcome to our afternoon meetings anymore, Nurse Sanders. And I've heard that you've not had any patients today. But I have to say, I think Mrs Brooks is absolutely right to protect her daughter and this community from...how shall I put it? Immoral influences.'

Suddenly the pieces fell into place. Paul had made good his threat and was out to destroy her. Summoning up all her strength, Connie stood tall. 'I don't think you are in any position to talk about morals, Paul. After all, who was it who had an affair with a married woman and was dismissed from the RCMP in disgrace?'

As soon as the words left her mouth, Connie knew she had made a mistake. She shouldn't have twisted the knife in a wound that was still not healed. If her own hurt was anything to go by, the pain would be great. It had been the wrong thing to do. She had lowered herself to his level. Connie cursed her hot-headedness as she walked past him, anger already dying, the flames doused by humiliation.

Connie no longer had the energy or will to tackle Mrs Brooks. She needed time to think. Time to calm her turbulent mind. Time to decide how to deal with this with a level head.

She couldn't afford a repeat of what had just happened with Paul.

Having put a pot of strong coffee on, she gazed at the static log fire, willing it to comfort her by moving and crackling. What was she doing here, sitting in front of a picture of a log fire, when she could have been back in Manchester enjoying the Christmas lights and the Salvation Army band, with her friends, followed by drinks in a cosy pub? She closed her eyes and breathed deeply, conjuring up the sights, smells and sounds of a Manchester Christmas.

Taking a few sips of coffee, Connie felt calmer and turning her gaze once more to the mural, reflected on the kindness and thoughtfulness of the friends who had spent the time making it for her. The warmth of these thoughts was better than the heat from any fire, and whatever the challenges in this world, she now had people in her life who cared about her just as she was. And this miraculous thing had happened here, in this white wilderness where people were few, and trust had to be earned. Connie was flattered that she had earned the generous friendship of this group of people. Leaning back against the cushions, sipping more coffee, Connie considered how she was going to tackle Mrs Brooks, and how she was going to regain the trust of the Inuit in the settlement.

Mrs Brooks set her mouth into a firm line when she saw Connie at the door, and for a moment Connie wondered whether she was going to even let her in.

'Mrs Brooks. I need to talk to you. It's important.' Connie kept her voice calm and made sure to look her adversary in the eye. Eventually, Mrs Brooks begrudgingly stepped aside and motioned for Connie to enter.

Once they were seated, both on the edges of their respective chintzy chairs. Connie took a deep breath.

'I understand from François that you no longer see me as a fit person to be around Esther. That is your decision to make, but I think at the very least you owe me an explanation.' Connie was astonished at this sudden calm authority that she had somehow gained. Where had that come from?

Mrs Brooks, her gaze fixed somewhere into the distance over Connie's left shoulder, refused to meet her eye. 'I misjudged you. I should never have let my guard down where you are concerned. Not for myself, and certainly not for Esther. The devil has put one of his own in our community,' she spat.

Connie couldn't disguise the gasp that escaped her. She had been called many things, but this was on a whole new level, and the anger of earlier was rekindled in a moment. 'And what makes you think that is the case?' She couldn't keep the ice out of her tone.

'You and that...Daisy. I know what you two have been up to, and it's...it's *disgusting*!'

'What, exactly, are you talking about?' Connie pinned Mrs Brooks gaze to hers.

Mrs Brooks had the grace to glance down at the floor an embarrassed flush creeping up her neck.

Connie swallowed and resisted the urge to call Mrs Brooks out on her nosiness and voyeuristic tendencies, but she would not repeat the mistake she had made with Paul. She wouldn't let her mouth run away with her this time, and clamped her lips shut,

Eventually Mrs Brooks lifted her head. 'Paul told me all about it, anyway. He is as shocked as I am.'

Connie clasped her hands tightly in her lap and willed herself to stay strong, and in control.

'First of all, you are mistaken in your...assumptions. Yes, Daisy did stay at my house. We had been talking late into the night, and it made sense for her to sleep on my settee and go home the next morning.' Connie didn't flinch at the lie, because in essence it was the truth. And she was not going to let Daisy become the topic of such toxic gossip. 'And secondly,' she continued, 'what I do within the four walls of my own home is none of your business. The Canadian government is my employer, not you. And you have no right to endanger the health of the people in this community by spreading malicious rumours. In addition,' Connie ploughed on, now in full flow, 'think about your daughter's happiness. You must have noticed a change in her since she has been working with Ilannaq. She felt useful and had a purpose. You gave that to her.' Connie felt proud of the kindness in the comment, and in some ways it was true. 'You must have noticed the benefit of the P.E. lessons. Physical exercise was doing her so much good, and she was having fun. You can't keep her locked up here.' Connie stopped remembering too late her promise to Rev Brooks, to tread gently. Maybe she had gone too far.

'How dare you lecture me about how to bring up my daughter!' Mrs Brooks stood, this time flushed with anger. 'How dare you be so insolent to your superiors. A slip of a girl like you, only just out of school!'

Connie, undaunted, stood, and using her height to tower over Mrs Brooks, said, 'I might be a slip of a girl, but I am a qualified nurse and I have responsibilities in this community that far outweigh yours.'

'Get out!' Mrs Brooks was shaking with rage. So much so that she could hardly get the words out.

Without responding. Connie headed for the door and escaped into the welcome cold of the white world outside.

# Chapter Twenty-Five

T his was a Christmas Day, the likes of which she would probably never have again. An adventure her grandfather would be proud of. Connie was desperately trying to put a positive slant on the way events had developed over the previous few weeks. After all that had happened, she was still here, and she wasn't giving up any time soon.

The four-hour snow mobile trip over mountainous terrain had jolted every bone in Connie's body and she had been aching and cold when she and the Inuit fishing party arrived at the fishing ground. In spite of her discomfort, she was impressed at the speed with which a camp was erected, the tents arranged around a fire. Once she was warm and had been fortified with bannock and tea, it had been time to rest. Not knowing or having any concept of time in this permanent darkness, Connie had simply slept until she was woken by the others. Once she had groggily adjusted to her surroundings, amazed, she saw that an igloo was under construction – the blocks of snow being deftly cut and shaped by the Inuit with their long, broad knives. 'This will be warmer than a tent when we are finished.' Moosasee grinned at her. 'Are you ready for jigging?'

Connie summoned up as much enthusiasm as she could and nodded vigorously, unsure quite what she was agreeing to, but assuming that 'jigging' had a different meaning here than at home. 'Okay.' She watched as he made a hole through the ice to the water using a machine-driven drill. Moosasee grinned and between his broken English and Connie's basic Inuktitut managed to communicate that in the past this would have been a lengthy process, done by hand with a long knife. He showed her the one he had stowed in their baggage, indicating that machinery could go wrong at any time, unlike the reliability of age-old methods and tools. Connie wondered how long the process would have taken by hand. She watched fascinated as he attached a lure of shiny paper to the line and slowly lowered it into the hole. He then handed her the line and mimed a jigging motion with his arm. Relieved that nothing more was required, Connie happily took over responsibility for the line.

She studied the landscape around her, for once not hidden in a snowstorm; but even so, it was difficult to make anything out in the near complete darkness. Instead, she listened to the silence, only broken by the low conversations between Moosasee and his fellow hunters. In the distance was the faint howling of wolves, but other than that there was nothing. For once, no howling wind. Connie became aware, trance-like, of her heart beating, oddly loud, in the silence.

Moosasee's hand was on her arm, moving it up and down, and Connie realised with a start that she had forgotten all about the jigging. She flashed him an apologetic smile and concentrated on the job in hand with renewed concentration.

She had learnt that Moosasee in fact spoke and understood much more English than he let on in the settlement, only revealing this to her when he had suggested the trip. Ilannaq had taken her to his home under the pretext of a medical problem, but once they arrived and had partaken of the inevitable tea,

Moosasee had turned to Connie and said, 'You? Fishing trip with us?'

Connie had turned to look at a grinning Ilannaq in confusion. 'He can speak some English, but it is better that they don't know. Sometimes he learns things when they forget he is there.' She tilted her head in the direction of Harbour Inlet.

Connie gave him with an admiring look, and then realised he was waiting for an answer to his invitation.

'Fishing? Me?'

Moosasee nodded. 'Yes, you.'

'We know that some people are not friendly with you, and we know why.'

As Connie looked at the floor in embarrassment, Moosasee touched her arm. 'Some of my people have taken to the Christian religion and do whatever the Brooks tell them. They have been told that you are of the devil, so they are afraid to come to your station.'

Connie felt tears of anger and humiliation prickle in her eyes and wiped them angrily with the back of her hand.

'But I do not agree. I believe that our traditions are better than the cruel Christianity with all that suffering and bad things. We do not worry about what people do with their bodies – we have more important concerns. You have been good to us, Nurse Sanders, and now it is time for us to be good to you.' His speech completed, Moosasee sat back on his heels with a smile.

'They would like to take you on Christmas Day, because they know it is a special day for you, a day for friends and family. They want to get you out of the settlement and make sure you are not alone.' Ilannaq gave her a nudge and a warm smile.

Connie was overwhelmed at the kindness and generosity of Ilannaq's family – and flattered. She knew that it was a very rare occurrence for a Westerner to be allowed anywhere near an Inuit fishing trip.

'Thank you, Moosasee. I am honoured,' she had said with as much gravitas as she could muster, aware, even so, of treacherous tears running down her cheeks.

And so, here she was. Connie Sanders, fishing in the Arctic with not a Westerner in sight, surrounded by the warmth and love of these people, and grateful for it.

A tug on the line interrupted her thoughts, although this time she had kept part of her mind on the task in hand. She gave a shout and Moosasee came over and showed her how to draw the line out and land her first cod. He patted her back in congratulation.

'For our girls, when they catch their first fish, they put it down their fronts, inside the clothes.' Connie couldn't disguise her horror, gasping and clapping her hand over her own chest. This was maybe a step too far in immersing herself in the Inuit culture.

Moosasee now joined by other members of the group laughed at her dismay. It ensures an easy birth when children are born. Koola, her baby safely cocooned in an *amauti* took her arm. 'Maybe not so successful for me, but at least my baby is here. Don't worry it is not for you to do. When I caught my first fish...' she held her nose in disgust.

'She stank for days,' her brother explained.

When a good number of cod had been stowed safely in the tent. Connie and her fellow fishers gathered around a fire in the igloo. Confused as to why the fire didn't melt the ice, she eventually understood that the minus-20-degree temperature outside turned any melting snow into ice, instantly, which only served to strengthen the structure. Sharing a meal of fresh cod, Connie had baulked at eating the raw fish that the others were tucking into with relish, and had managed to cook some over the fire, much to the amusement of her companions. She didn't need to prove herself to Ilannaq's family now, knowing they would respect her preference for cooked fish, and take it in good part. Connie felt safer and happier than she had for many years, in the middle of this immense white wasteland. It was the best Christmas dinner that she could ever remember.

After they had slept, head to tail in the igloo, there was more fishing, until eventually, Moosasee indicated that they had enough and that it was time to return.

The return journey was even more gruelling than the journey out but the Inuit seemed unfazed, having an uncanny sense of how to get home, with the help of the few dogs they had brought with them. Connie smiled as she remembered childhood trips to Cornwall where her mother and father had argued over large, ungainly paper maps, often ending up taking the Ford Anglia down ever-narrowing lanes. Only when David took over from their mother, navigating from the front seat did they eventually reach the sea.

A herd of caribou could be seen approaching, seemingly unaware of the downwind hunting party. Although she had made her peace with this aspect of the Inuit culture, actually seeing an animal slaughtered before her eyes was something Connie didn't know if she could endure. She sat rigid, hardly daring to breathe, clutching the handlebars of the skidoo, willing the magnificent animals to somehow sense their presence and run. She knew her thinking was irrational, because caribou meat, skin and horns were essential for the Inuit way of life, but she somehow couldn't join up the logic with her instinctive emotions. The minutes seem to turn into an age as Connie grappled with her conflicted feelings.

Then a pack of Arctic wolves, also sensing the herd of caribou could be seen approaching from their left, anxious to join the party. Once the wolves had been spotted, the Inuit lowered their guns. 'We have enough, and will let nature take its course,' said Moosasee starting up his skidoo. Connie had never been so relieved.

By the time the lights of Harbour Inlet came into sight, Connie had lost all feeling in her feet and toes, and her face was burning in spite of the snow goggles and face covering. She stumbled and fell when she dismounted from the skidoo and had the strange sensation that her feet were no longer attached to her body. Moosasee sent someone to fetch Ilannaq.

After a rapid conversation where they reverted to Inuktitut, Ilannaq turned to Connie. 'Let's get you warm. My father thinks you have – what do you call it – bitten by the cold?'

'Frost bite.' Connie managed to get out between her chattering teeth. Having given Moosasee and her fellow travellers a weak smile and a wave. Connie allowed Ilannaq to lead her indoors to a strong, hot, coffee.

Ilannaq quickly and efficiently removed all of the coverings from Connie's feet and legs, examining them carefully. 'Your feet are frozen, a bit,' she pronounced eventually.

'A bit?' Connie reached down to her numb feet and sensed that her toes did indeed feel hard and something like the frozen fish stored in the Bay shop. Alarmed, she turned to Ilannaq. 'What should I do? Will I be okay?'

Ilannaq sat beside her and took her hand. 'You will be fine, but you must not let your feet warm too quickly.' Gesturing towards the painting, she grinned and said, 'A pretend fire is perfect.'

She turned back to Connie. 'You need painkillers, because when your feet and toes warm up, they will be painful and you might get some blisters.' Connie recalled the itchy, painful chilblains that came with the damp cold of Manchester that had been made worse by sitting too close to the coal fire. She nodded.

'I'll get you some and you rest,' Ilannaq commanded as she left.

# Chapter Twenty-Six

A fter several days of not being able to put any weight on her feet, Connie eventually felt stable enough to walk around the house. Once she could bear the feel of socks and then *kamiks* on her feet, she set off for the Nurse's Station, determined to get back to work after her enforced Christmas break.

It seemed that an uneasy truce had come into effect. Over the next few weeks she had a few patients, whose pain or discomfort drove them to ignore the dire warnings of hell put about by Mrs Brooks, but she saw no sign of Esther or the Brooks themselves. Moosasee's influence still carried weight in the community, though, and Connie was relieved that she was still able to continue with the TB programme, at least.

She avoided the Hudson Bay office wherever possible, quailing under the icy hatred of Paul Archer and the leering grins and lewd comments of the other men. On her previous, essential visit to use the radio, she had been greeted with loud whispers and from the less inhibited, comments such as, 'You'll get over it when you've had a good seeing to.' or 'What's it like? Can I watch?' Fortunately, Jim had appeared and sternly reminded the men that they had work to do. Connie was grateful, but there was no mistaking the intention of the touch of his hand on the lower part of her back as he ushered her to the radio.

'How are things in Manchester? I'll bet you miss Borough Market.'

Connie moved away and sat down, but nevertheless felt the least she could do was to talk to him after he had rescued her without making any further comment about the toxic rumours.

'Yes, I used to go there with my mum. She bought all her veg there, and I had to help her carry it all home.' Connie laughed, grateful to share common memories in spite of Jim's thinly disguised ulterior motives. 'And what I would give for some Friday night fish and chips from the chippy – and batter scraps. We used to go in and stand on tiptoes to reach the counter and shout "Got any batter scraps, mister?"'

'I can just imagine it.' Jim said. 'What would Manchester Friday nights be like without fish and chips? My mum used to send me with a jug to the Outside Beer to get beer for my dad. Do you remember Barmy Mick at Cross Lane Market?' Jim leant forward as he warmed to his theme.

'God, yes! "I give you not one...not two...but four of these lovely plates."' Connie found herself slipping effortlessly into the impersonation, and they both laughed, as she stretched out her arm, imitating Barmy Mick's trick of balancing the aforesaid plates along the length of his arm. 'How did he do that?'

'God knows. It's so wonderful to talk to someone from the same world as me,' Jim said with fervour after a pause. 'Who would have thought I'd go all the way to the Canadian Arctic and end up talking about Barmy Mick?' Abruptly changing the subject, he asked, 'What do you make of Her Ladyship? Who would have thought the likes of us would be living in the same place as a duke's daughter!'

'I know what you mean, but she seems okay from what I know so far.'

'You know her family didn't approve of her marrying below her status. They wouldn't want us "common people" — Jim made speech marks in the air – contaminating their bloodline. Apparently, it was Tom's plan for them to escape her world, and come somewhere thousands of miles away, away from her family, where they could be a normal couple.' Jim leant forward with a conspiratorial air. 'Between you and me, I think he wanted to be somewhere where he was the king pin and not Kathy. She seems happy playing second in command at the school though.'

Much as she had enjoyed the gossip and the reminiscences, Connie didn't feel that she wanted to prolong the conversation any further or risk getting into anything more personal. The familiar pain of homesickness was lurking on the edges of her mind. 'Okay, I'd better get on and make this call. Thanks, Jim for...back there.' Feeling that she done enough to repay her debt, and becoming increasingly aware of Jim's hand creeping around her shoulder, Connie decided that she had had enough of Memory Lane and the British obsession with social class.

Over the next few weeks Connie spent several mornings sharing a coffee with Kathy and enjoyed her company, eventually forgetting all about her titled status. It seemed that Kathy was glad to have a fellow conspirator – someone with whom to gang up with against the Brooks, and it became apparent that she had been harbouring a deep resentment towards Mrs Brooks in particular for some time, after she had voiced disapproval of their partying lifestyle. And Connie allowed herself to be swept along on a temptingly soothing tide of self-pity and resentment.

'Bloody hypocrites, the lot of them,' Kathy sneered. 'It was bad enough back home being made to go to church every Sunday to be forced to listen to the supposed wisdom of that lecherous old vicar we had.'

It seemed almost too easy, and Connie found herself joining in with the sniping and sneering – enhanced even further when Tom was around. Connie came to learn that he and Paul Archer had a long-standing feud, and Tom was scathing about the way the Hudson Bay was run. Kathy and Tom were all for the cooperative as a way for the Inuit to sell their carvings, but Connie realised over time that it was less about what was good for the Inuit, and more about getting one up on Paul Archer. Perceived wrongs had long shadows in small settlements, it seemed.

The only other ray of sunshine in the darkness was the fun they had on film nights, held whenever the weather permitted, followed by drinks with Thierry and François. Connie was sad that Esther was never seen at any of them, and worried about how she was doing. She did confide in François, however, her sadness about the demise of the dancing lessons. After Connie and Esther had been banned, it seemed that somehow things weren't the same and the enthusiasm had fizzled out. Connie sensed that she missed Esther's company, although nothing seemed to dampen François's spirits for long – not even the endless winter days. She seemed incapable of the brooding anger and resentment of those around her and appeared to thrive in a world of romance novels and any film magazines she could get her family to send. As long as she was with her man François was happy it seemed, and selling her pastries in the Bay shop had given her a new purpose.

Tom's long-awaited moment of triumph came at last, when, after several months he found out who had been fiddling the books at the Hudson Bay depot. Being a maths graduate, Tom, when he wasn't teaching, had been hired to audit the Hudson Bay books and accounts once a year, and had made no secret of the fact to Kathy and Connie that he had found discrepancies in the figures. He had gleefully sworn them to silence as he investigated further, and Connie got the feeling that he was banking on the fact that Paul would be the culprit. Over the next few weeks, stalking his prey with endless patience and precision, Tom became more animated than Connie had ever seen him. Gone was the morose, brooding character who had arrived in June.

Connie had always felt sorry for the children in the settlement school having such a bad-tempered teacher, but she was reassured by Kathy and François that once he was in front of a class of children, an enthusiastic and inspirational teacher emerged, 'like a butterfly from a chrysalis,' François had said, miming the action with her arms, making her and Kathy laugh. Connie vowed to pay the school a visit one day and see this supposed phenomenon for herself.

After several more weeks of observation and forensic accounting, it was discovered and proven that the culprit was, in fact, Jim Briggs. Tom's disappointment was tempered by the fact that this fraud had happened under Paul's watch, and he had wasted no time in sending a report to Montreal recommending that the station was to receive regular external audits.

Jim was rapidly dispatched back to the mainland without ceremony, a sorry figure trudging to the plane with only a duffel bag containing his few belongings. Connie wondered how he would find life back in Manchester. Apparently, he was going back to live with his mother. Connie couldn't imagine any good outcome for Jim after this, and even felt a bit sorry for him. In fact, as time went by, she began to tire of the endless gloating and sniping, and almost felt ashamed that she had allowed herself to be sucked in, to what was becoming a toxic mix of heavy drinking, gossiping and downright unkind conversation.

She began to spend more time on her own, reading, or writing in her journal, and even trying her hand at poetry. After all, how many other people of her age would have had the experiences that she had? Maybe one day, her ramblings would provide an interesting glimpse back into a time and way of life that she knew was, even then, rapidly disappearing.

She and Oliver fell into the habit of sharing a drink once a week. Connie enjoyed his friendship, and even though she didn't want to admit it, part of her felt that it would do no harm to be seen spending time in male company.

One evening, Connie couldn't resist the temptation to try out Daisy's line. 'So come on, Oliver. Why are you really here? What are you running away from? We're all running from something.'

Oliver had given a simple one-word answer: 'Conscription.'

As nothing else seemed forthcoming, Connie pressed further. 'Yes, just like several of your "colleagues" who are fleeing the US military machine.' She mimed quotes. 'But why?'

Oliver sighed and leant forward, his elbows resting on his legs, avoiding Connie's gaze. 'I guess you think we're all cowards.' When Connie didn't answer, he continued. 'But I'm not. For me, it's... I just couldn't live that life, and I couldn't kill people. I think it's wrong. And if I shot someone dead, it would haunt me for the rest of my life. I know it would.'

He looked up at Connie as she grasped his hand and squeezed it. 'Of course I don't think you're a coward. You have principles...and it takes courage to make a stand against something you don't think is right.'

'I wish my family agreed with you. They were so ashamed, they told me not to ever come home again.'

Connie gasped, keeping a tight hold of his hand. 'Oh my God. Oliver,' was all she could say.

'So I ran and ended up here, along with all the other draft-dodgers.' He gave a wry laugh. 'I know I wouldn't last five minutes in the army, I'm not like that. What I really want to do is to study art.' Oliver paused, glancing at the warm colours of the fire. 'Maybe I will one day.'

Connie pulled the lemon dressing gown around her, folding her arms to hold it in place. 'You remind me so much of my brother, David. That's all he wants to do, too. But of course my parents wouldn't hear of it, and now he's studying law at university.'

'Even so, he'll probably settle down, get married and have children one day, and they'll be proud of him. I know that's never going to happen for me. Not if I'm honest with myself.'

'Me neither.'

He looked at Connie and she held his gaze as they shared a moment of mutual understanding. 'We're the same.' Connie couldn't find the language to describe their situation, but nevertheless the unspoken communication was clear. Encouraged, she shared what had happened with Helen and found to her surprise that the story was getting easier to tell each time and noticed, once again, that the tight ball of hurt, humiliation and anger that she had arrived with took up less space in her mind, now.

'I hope you don't mind me saying, but it must be hard all these rumours about you and Daisy.' This time it was Oliver's turn to squeeze Connie's hand.

'Yup. Not easy. But I've just put my head down and tried to get on as best I can.' She sat back and sighed. 'And I'm so lucky to have the support of Ilannaq and her family.' She gave a rueful laugh.

'What will you do when Daisy comes back?' It was a simple enough question.

Connie thought. 'I don't know.' She had put off thinking about it, because she really didn't know. In fact, she had heard very little from Daisy, but it seemed that her mother did not have long to live. She requested that Connie continue to collect and catalogue the carvings, taking a photo to accompany each one. Connie had immersed herself in the project, and it seemed that, gradually, trust was returning among the Inuit, apart from a group of converts who were staunch in their attendance at Bible studies and prayer meetings – led in Inuktitut by Rev Brooks. This group avoided any contact, even moving away from Connie if they saw her, as if she had the plague.

She had seen Rev Brooks a few times, and he had simply passed her with a curt nod. She sensed that he was disappointed in her. This distressed her more than his wife's anger in a strange way. She'd had thought they had a rapport.

The uncomfortable atmosphere in the settlement festered on for a few more weeks, until, one morning, very imperceptibly, there was a lighter area in the sky. Connie wondered if she was imagining it, but on arriving at the Nurse's Station she sensed Ilannaq's excitement. 'The sun is coming soon,' she pronounced, eyes shining. And the atmosphere seemed to transform into a sense of anticipation, as, each day the sky became tinged with reds, yellows and oranges.

# Chapter
# Twenty-Seven

A s the sky was getting lighter, but before the sun appeared, Daisy returned in a flurry of blue bags, parcels,
and information for Moosasee about the success of the newly
fledged cooperative. Connie hadn't received any warning of
her arrival and was consumed with anxiety about how Daisy
would react to the dark developments that had happened
since she had been away. Most of all, she didn't want Daisy
to be hurt by the malicious lies, but she was also worried that
it would put an end to their friendship. Maybe she wouldn't
want to have anything more to do with Connie. Maybe she
would want to distance herself from such a pariah. Connie
realised that there was still a lot about Daisy that she didn't
know. You don't know someone's true nature until you see
them in a crisis, or when their loyalty was put to the test. She
had learnt that the hard way when Helen had crumbled under
the same scrutiny and headed for marriage as fast as she could.
Would Daisy be the same? She didn't know.

All these thoughts swirled around in Connie's head as she
watched the plane land on the still-stable sea ice.

Daisy approached and enveloped her in a hug, but feeling Connie stiffen, she stepped away. 'Sorry, I just...' She hesitated, before picking up her bag and striding off. Connie feeling the watchful eyes of most of the settlement on them, fought to conceal the tears that threatened to overwhelm her. Why had she done that? *Why?* She'd been so busy thinking of Daisy's loyalty, when maybe it was her own that was in question. In some way, she'd not wanted to give people the chance to tar Daisy with the same brush as they had her, but if Connie was honest, she knew they already did. She berated herself for her cowardice and trudged to the Nurse's Station.

The following day, everyone looked in awe and excitement as the first rays of sun appeared, casting an orange glow on the horizon. Trying to capture the moment with her camera, Connie turned to find Daisy at her side.

Plunging in, she said, 'Daisy, I'm so sorry about your mother.' When there was no reply, Connie turned to face Daisy. 'I mean it, I am so sorry Daisy. You must have been through a terrible time.'

'If you are ashamed to be seen with me, the least you could do is admit it.' Connie could just make out the words Daisy muttered under her breath.

'What? No! What are you talking about!' Connie felt a twinge of guilt at the lie. Her knee-jerk reaction when she'd felt all eyes on them could not be undone. But she ploughed on regardless: 'I just didn't want to make things worse...for you.'

'Oh come on! You could at least be honest. Don't tell me you weren't concerned for yourself as well.' Daisy cut through Connie's soft, self-delusion with words of ice.

'You weren't here to deal with all the toxic gossip, though, were you? I've had to put up with being ignored and made fun of – you haven't.' Connie could feel her anger and self-justification growing.

'Yes, I heard about the gossip and rumours about us – the ripples have even reached Frobisher Bay thanks to Ma Brooks and the Hudson Bay grapevine.' Daisy moved her foot in the snow making a fan shaped indent. 'But I never took you for someone who would bow under that kind of gossip. I thought you were a fighter against all injustice. You've always been so quick to judge others.'

Connie felt the full force of the below-the-belt accusation and knew deep down that Daisy had a point. And then she reverted to the only way she knew to deal with hurt and humiliation – to put a distance between herself and the cause. 'I think it's best all round to give each other a wide berth, don't you?' Connie tried to keep the tremor from her voice, and moved away, striding towards the Nurse's Station. And she'd worried about Daisy not wanting to have anything to do with *her*? How had things turned on their head so quickly?

She saw very little of Daisy over the following few weeks, busying herself with work and photography. Now that there was a market for the Inuit carvings, she took great pride in taking the photos to go with them. She learnt via Ilannaq and Moosasee that more of the elders had now been persuaded to join the scheme, but, even so, she decided to avoid the second meeting where Daisy had filled them all in on the details, pleading pressure of work.

The following morning, Ilannaq arrived and without preamble said, 'Where were you last night? Why weren't you at the meeting? I know you did not have work to do!' She fixed Connie with a stern gaze.

'I...I just don't want to add to any more gossip. It's best if Daisy and I are not seen together.'

'But don't you realise that you are making things worse?' Ilannaq shook her head in frustration. 'It looks as if you are hiding something, as if you are ashamed. My people see that as a weakness. Most of them had no problem with you and Daisy, but now they have a problem with *you*. You are siding with the Westerners and their values.'

Connie felt the heat of shame rise up through her body to her face. She hadn't thought through about how it would look; she'd just grabbed the solution that had suited her own needs and had tried to justify it with flimsy excuses. Tears welling in her eyes, she turned and made to go through the records for that day.

'So what are you going to do?' For the first time in their friendship, Connie detected real anger and hurt in Ilannaq's tone.

She looked up. 'Do? What can I do? The damage is done.' Had she really turned into this unattractive self-pitying, whining person that she already detested from outside of herself.

'The damage can be undone,' said Ilannaq firmly. 'Go and make up with Daisy. Show that you are not ashamed of your...friend, or yourself.' She added in a gentler tone, 'Show my people, and yourself, that you are stronger than this.'

Connie approached Daisy's dwelling with trepidation. She had never been there and was surprised that it was nothing more than a makeshift hut. They had always met at Connie's house and Connie had never questioned it. She was hoping that Daisy wouldn't be there so that she could creep back knowing that she could tell Ilannaq that at least she'd tried.

But a few minutes after Connie's tentative knock, just as she was turning away, relief rising in her heart, the door opened.

'I thought you said we should avoid each other. I've kept my end of the bargain.' The hardness in Daisy's voice made Connie squirm in embarrassment.

'Can I come in?' Her impression of a makeshift home was confirmed as Connie took in the one-roomed hut. There was nothing of any permanence, nothing that couldn't be packed into a few bags at short notice. No books, photos, pictures, nothing.

'Now you can see why it was always better for me to come to yours. I don't do permanence, and I prefer memories to be made elsewhere, not where I live. I don't want any baggage, emotional or otherwise in my life.'

There was an angry bitterness that brought tears to Connie's eyes. Had she been so concerned with protecting herself from hurt that she hadn't even thought about the pain she might have caused Daisy? She had always seemed so confident and strong.

'Daisy, I...' Connie took a breath, unsure how to continue. She'd convinced herself that Daisy wouldn't have been in and hadn't given much thought to what she would say if she was.

Daisy looked at her, head on one side, waiting.

'I... Oh God, I've made such a mess of things, and I don't know how to sort anything out.' To her horror, Connie found herself sobbing.

She was aware of Daisy's arm around her, leading her to the bed. She drew up the single chair and sat opposite Connie, warming her heart as she lifted her head tucking a strand of hair behind her ear.

'It's okay. We'll sort it out, Connie. And I'm sorry – I guess it was my turn to be over-judgemental this time. I'm sorry.'

'I'll bet not many people get to hear you say that.' Connie managed a smile as the tears ran down her cheeks. Eventually she broke the silence. 'I thought...I don't know what I thought would happen when you got back. And even though I told Mrs...Ma Brooks what I thought of her gossipmongering, somehow, when you were actually there in front of me, I felt everyone watching, and I was a coward. I'm sorry.'

'I guess that makes us even in the apology stakes.' Daisy gave Connie a smile that turned her insides to jelly. 'I think we both need coffee with some fortification – for medicinal purposes, of course.'

Connie followed Daisy's every move as she rustled up the welcome drinks in her Campingaz kitchen.

'I really am sorry about your mother, Daisy.'

Daisy didn't answer until they were both settled, Connie on the bed propped up with cushions and Daisy on the chair. Then she let out a long, slow breath as if she was decompressing after a long struggle.

'I can't say it's been easy, but I'm glad I was there.'

'Were your brothers around to help?'

'Not really, three of them live overseas with families of their own, and my youngest brother, Ted is...he has Downes syndrome.'

Connie sat forward, looking at Daisy in consternation. 'I had no idea – oh, Daisy...'

'Actually, Ted's been the least of my problems. He's very active, has his own friends and even holds down a part-time job at a local café. He's been living in supervised accommodation for a while and loves the independence. Like me, he's never felt particularly close to our mother, but even so, it's still been a blow for him. Luckily he has wonderful, supportive friends and a great social worker.'

Daisy leant back in the chair and took a sip of coffee. 'I don't know how much Ted realised, but my mother was embarrassed by him – the afterthought following a brood of four healthy children. He's lived in residential accommodation since he was small, conveniently out of sight.' There was a touch of bitterness and anger in Daisy's tone.

'But it sounds like he's happy in the life he has, so that's good, isn't it?'

'Yes, it is. Like I said, he's been the least of my problems...'

'So how was it, spending time with your mother?' Connie prompted.

'Not easy, is the short answer. She was angry, refusing to accept that there was anything wrong when I got there, saying that it was a lot of fuss about nothing. She almost seemed annoyed that I was there at all.' Daisy sighed. 'But it was soon obvious that the cancer was taking hold and each day she was able to do less and less. Her so-called friends stopped calling when it became too challenging to see one of their own dying – as if death was getting a bit too close for comfort. When it was too much for her to get up the stairs, reality sank in, and it was just awful to watch her lose her fighting spirit. I got her a place in a hospice, and she just accepted it without any comment – just went along with whatever the doctors said. It was almost like she wasn't my mother anymore. In lots of ways, at that point, I wished the old, snobbish, overbearing person she had always been, would come back.' Daisy wiped her eyes with the back of her sleeve.

'Come here.' Connie moved and made space for Daisy on the bed beside her. Daisy climbed on to the bed, all arms and legs, and settled beside Connie, who put an arm around her and held her close.

'The weird thing was that in the last few weeks, she became happier and somehow more peaceful. We talked about what I do up here, and for the first time she was genuinely interested. "I'm proud of you Daisy," is what she said.' Daisy stifled a sob. 'And she also said she was sorry for trying to make me do something that wasn't right for me, for encouraging me to marry Ralph. That all her life she'd tried to please people – keep up appearances, but in the end, where had it got her? The friends she'd had soon deserted her when anything more than gossip and small talk was required. But the amazing thing was that she wasn't angry or bitter, but more wondering. Somehow curious that she'd never realised it before.'

Connie squeezed Daisy's shoulder.

'So, at the end, she died at peace with herself and the world, and I'm so glad we were able to get to know each other at last. That's the mother I'm going to remember.'

They sat in a comfortable silence, Connie not wanting to intrude on Daisy's thoughts with easy platitudes.

Eventually, when Connie could no longer feel her arm, she shifted, and Daisy sat up. 'Time for another drink, I think,' she said, jumping off the bed.

'I'm really worried about Esther,' Connie said as Daisy handed her a mug of coffee. 'I haven't seen her at all – it's almost like her mother is keeping her prisoner.'

Apparently, Esther's lessons with Ilannaq were still held at the Brooks's house, but under the ever-present, watchful eye of her mother. Ilannaq had said that she was worried about how withdrawn the girl had become. 'She is unhappy, like a prisoner,' Ilannaq had said.

Connie felt powerless to intervene, but nevertheless felt she should do something. Belatedly, she had shared Esther's secret hiding place with Ilannaq, warning her that Esther might ask her to cover her absence. Connie felt a pang of remorse that she hadn't spoken to Ilannaq before and then gone to reassure Esther that her secret would be safe. Now it was too late.

'I feel sorry for her, having that woman as a mother.' Daisy blew the steam over her hot drink.

'I'm wondering whether I should go over to the Brooks's and try to make some kind of contact. But I don't think she'd even let me over the threshold!'

'Probably just as well. You'd be playing with fire there, Connie. Best not to poke your nose into other people's family problems.'

Connie huffed in exasperation. 'But I'm worried.'

'I know, and I do feel sorry for Esther, but I'm not sure that it's a problem for us to sort out.'

# Chapter
# Twenty-Eight

C onnie, in spite of Daisy's warning, was determined to do something to help Esther – she couldn't just stand by and do nothing. So before her courage failed her, she found herself face-to-face with Mrs Brooks the following morning.

'You've got a nerve!' the older woman snarled.

Connie wondered about how a Christian could act in such an un-Jesus-like way but put the thought to the back of her mind – that was for another day.

'I need to speak to your husband about the Inuit cooperative,' said Connie firmly. She had invented the excuse on the way over.

'He's a busy man. But I'll tell him you called.' Connie could almost see the gritted teeth.

'Are you saying that I can't see him?' Connie was not going to let this go without a fight.

'As I said, he is busy. Now if you don't mind...' And with that she slammed the door in Connie's face.

She trudged back to the Nurse's Station and having treated a few patients, shared her concerns once again with Ilannaq.

'I tried to get in to see Rev Brooks, but Mrs Brooks wouldn't let me in. I don't know what else we can do.'

'I can tell she is very unhappy. I feel so sorry for her.'

'It's not right to stop her from having friends and seeing people. She's at the age when she should be enjoying life.' Connie tried to tamp down the anger and frustration she felt.

'Don't worry. At least I get to see her, and I'll keep an eye out.'

Connie headed for home, to find Daisy already there and conjuring up a meal.

'Goodness. You can actually cook? You've kept that quiet!' Connie joked as she took off her parka. 'But whatever it is, it smells good.'

'Arctic kedgeree,' announced Daisy. 'Cod, rice and pow-dered egg. Coming up.' She started to spoon the steaming contents of the pan onto two plates. 'I thought it was the least I could do after making you listen to all my angst last night.'

'You've done the same for me...and it's what friends do...real friends, that is.'

Daisy didn't comment, but signalled for Connie to dig in.

Afterwards, contented and full, they settled on the settee – now returned to its summer position facing the window and enjoyed the growing daylight.

Connie broke the silence. 'I visited the Brooks's today, but as expected, I was given short shrift and told by Mrs Brooks, in no uncertain terms, to never darken their door again.' She sighed. 'At least I tried. Ilannaq says she'll keep an eye on Esther, but it's difficult when her mother is always there.'

Daisy gave her a stern look. 'I know, I know I it's none of my business, but even so...'

They sat in silence for a few minutes looking out over the bay, the weak sun now turning everything to a pale blush of pink.

'I've got quite a few films to get developed, so when the next flight comes in, I'll send them off. Do you think we should send some carvings too? Or maybe wait until you go back to the mainland so you can deliver them in person.'

'I don't trust anybody from the Bay, or the pilots for that matter. The pieces could easily "get lost". I think we'll wait until I can take them myself.'

Daisy was just getting ready to go when the phone rang once. She paused, hat in hand, as Connie lifted the receiver to hear the RCMP call.

'I know everyone in Harbour Inlet is listening, and we need your help. Esther Brooks has not been seen for over an hour, and no one knows her whereabouts.' Connie took a sharp intake of breath. Daisy came over and they listened, holding the receiver between them. 'We're assembling a search party outside the church.' There was a pause, before the RCMP officer spoke again. 'It goes without saying that we need to find her quickly.'

Connie and Daisy rushed to get ready and headed for the church where a small crowd of both Westerners and Inuit had already gathered.

Connie, seeing Rev Brooks in deep discussion with the RCMP officer and Paul Archer, turned to search out Mrs Brooks. She was standing alone, and as Connie approached she was shocked at how much she seemed to have shrunk in on herself, and felt a pang of sympathy. This woman had alienated so many people that she had no one to turn to in her hour of need. Connie approached. No matter how much Mrs Brooks had made her life difficult, she couldn't begin to imagine what she was going through now.

'Mrs Brooks, I...'

The older woman looked up and the distress Connie had briefly seen hid itself behind a mask of anger.

'How dare you come here!' And in a louder voice she shouted, 'I wouldn't be surprised if you've got something to do with this. It's the devil's work.'

Rev Brooks strode over, and in an effort to calm his wife, said gently, 'This isn't the time, Martha.'

'I will not have these women anywhere near my daughter. I forbid them to take part.'

Silence descended on the group, as Daisy stepped forward. 'Whatever your feelings about Connie and me, surely you need all the help you can get, Mrs Brooks. Maybe it's time to put our disagreements behind us – at least for now.'

The heavy silence was broken by Mrs Brooks. 'I forbid it!'

The RCMP officer took Daisy and Connie to one side. 'I think we have to abide by the family's wishes. I think it's best that you go.'

'But...' Connie protested.

'Come on.' Daisy took Connie's arm. 'Let's go.'

Once they were a few hundred yards away, Connie suddenly stopped and turned to face Daisy. 'I've had a thought. I think I know where she might have gone. I need to find Ilannaq.'

They found her at the Nurse's Station. 'I thought I would prepare things for Esther. She might need treatment when they find her.' Anxiety was etched into her face. She and Esther had grown close, and like Connie, she had been worried about her child teacher.

'Ilannaq, did Esther tell you that she was going to her secret place?'

Ilannaq turned, wide-eyed. 'How could she?'

'I thought maybe she might have found a way...' Connie tailed off, again cursing herself for letting Esther down.

Connie could see distress growing on Ilannaq's face.

'I think she's gone to her secret place. It seems the obvious thing. Daisy and I will go and look. You prepare sutures, antibiotics and painkillers.'

Connie drew Ilannaq into a hug. 'What would I do without you?'

'Where is she?' Daisy asked as they prepared to leave.

'Ages ago she told me about a cave near Cooper's Pond that she went to when she wanted to be alone. I told her to always tell Ilannaq if she was going there in case anything happened. But...' Connie shook her head in exasperation. 'I forgot to tell Ilannaq, and let Esther know she could trust her. I told her to never go there without telling someone – me or Ilannaq, but in the end she couldn't say anything, because her mother was always there! It's all my fault.'

Daisy placed both of her hands on Connie's shoulders and looked her in the eye. 'It is not all your fault. Esther made that decision, knowing it would be dangerous. And anyway, playing the blame game isn't going to help anybody at this point.'

Connie hung her head. 'You're right. It's not about me. This is about saving Esther.'

'Let's get going and hope you're right about where she went.' Daisy put her arm around Connie and gave her a squeeze. 'Follow me, I know where Cooper's Pond is, and it's less than a mile. Shouldn't take long.'

Hurrying through the thin spring light, they slowed as they neared the melting ice on the pond's surface. Connie's stomach twisted at the thought of how deathly cold the water would be. If Esther had somehow fallen into the pond, she would never have survived. Before she could think further, Daisy grabbed her arm. 'You said something about a cave. It shouldn't be too difficult to find. You go that way and I'll go this way and we'll meet over there.' She indicated the far side of the pond. 'Take this whistle.'

'What about you?'

Daisy's answer was an ear-splitting whistle that erupted through fingers placed in her mouth. 'I didn't have four brothers without learning to do that.'

They listened for any answering sound but heard nothing. 'Right see you on the other side.' Connie could see Daisy's wild blonde hair escaping from under the red bobble hat as she strode off. There was no one else she would have wanted to help her in this crisis, and below the brusque, no-nonsense front, Connie now knew Daisy well enough to know that she was as anxious as any of them about Esther's fate.

Setting off around the other side of the pond, Connie searched the permafrost for any signs of a hiding place or a cave. There were no trees and very little vegetation, and Daisy was right, a cave should be easy to spot. Jogging soon turned to walking after Connie, stooping, hands on knees had paused to catch her breath. They had covered nearly all the ground and she was beginning to think she must have been mistaken when a shrill whistle broke her thoughts. Heart pumping, Connie raced towards the sound, breathlessness forgotten. She saw the red hat low to the ground, as if Daisy was crouching over something, and stifling a sob, she threw herself forwards.

Daisy was at the entrance to a small rocky structure, too small to be called a cave. As Connie drew nearer, she heard Daisy talking. 'It's alright, Esther, we've got you. Connie's here.'

'Esther!' Connie, knelt, breathless. 'It's okay, sweetheart, we've got you.'

Esther's mouth moved, but no sound emerged, and Connie's medical instincts took over.

'Can you get her to drink something?' she asked Daisy.

Daisy coaxed Esther into a sitting position and wrapped a blanket they had brought around the girl before putting a water bottle to her lips. As she did so, she silently inclined her head towards Esther's leg.

Connie gently removed the sock and with a pair of scissors from her bag and cut the trouser leg. A long open wound ran along the leg from Esther's knee to her ankle. Dressing it with a temporary bandage from the first-aid kit they had brought, Connie said, 'We need to get her back to the Nurse's Station before this gets infected.'

'Esther, can you walk between us? We're going to get you home.'

A weak nod and Connie and Daisy took an arm each, and between them managed to half-carry Esther back to the settlement. Connie had never been as glad of Daisy's strong physique – there was no way she could have got Esther back on her own. And if she had left her there while she went for help— Connie shivered at the thought.

# Chapter
# Twenty-Nine

A s soon as they arrived, Ilannaq leapt into action, helping them to place Esther gently on the bed. 'You should go to the Bay and let them know Esther is safe,' Connie said to Daisy, who, hovering by the bed, seemed suddenly overwhelmed by the situation now that the urgency was over.

'Daisy...' Connie put her hand on Daisy's arm. Daisy blinked as she dragged her gaze away from Esther.

'Right. Yes, of course.' She spoke hurriedly before heading for the door.

Connie found herself with a new sense of authority and calmly examined Esther, who was still only just conscious, for any other injuries.

'Does it hurt anywhere else, Esther?'

With great effort, the girl shook her head. 'Am I going to die?'

'You're safe now, and once I've patched you up, you'll be as good as new.' Connie summoned up her most positive bedside manner. 'You've got a nasty cut on your leg, so I'm going to numb the pain and then stitch you back together.'

Without any prompting, Ilannaq held Esther's hand and kept her talking while Connie injected the local anaesthetic and inspected the wound. It was clean but deep, and Connie suspected Esther had fallen and cut it on one of the jagged rocks around the cave. She stitched, slowly and carefully wanting to avoid as much scarring as possible.

Just as she had finished, the door burst open and Mrs Brooks rushed in. Ignoring Ilannaq and Connie she went to Esther and held her, stooping awkwardly over the bed. Between sobs of relief, Connie could detect an edge of anger as she said, 'Where have you *been*?' When Esther didn't respond, she continued, 'You've had us all so worried!'

Rev Brooks appeared and took his daughter's hand, squeezing it, unable to speak. Connie and Ilannaq stood back to give them some space and while Ilannaq cleaned the equipment, Connie surveyed the tableaux of this strange and dysfunctional family united in relief.

Eventually Rev Brooks turned to Connie. 'You have saved our daughter's life. You and Daisy. How can we ever thank you?'

Connie stiffened in anticipation as Mrs Brooks rose to her feet. Rev Brooks, equally alarmed, said, 'Come on, Martha. She has saved Esther's life,' as he stood and took her hand.

Connie couldn't read Mrs Brooks's face. She turned to her husband. 'It's all right, Richard. I know what I need to say.'

She turned to Connie and took a deep breath. 'Daisy told us where you found Esther. I think you knew where to find her because she confided in you. Am I right?'

'Mrs Brooks, I—'

Mrs Brooks held up her hand, cutting Connie short. 'I know she went off sometimes, but I also knew that if I asked her where she was going, she would become even more secretive. I'm the one to blame here, I'm the one who drove her to this.'

She sat suddenly and bowed her head. 'I knew I was losing her to you, to François, to the world, and I couldn't stop it. But she is all I have.'

Connie's heart clenched with pity for the broken woman before her.

The silence was broken by Esther. 'I'm sorry.'

Her mother took Esther's hand in both of her own and looked into her eyes. 'It's alright, Esther. I'm the one who should be sorry.' Her voice trembled, as her head remained bowed.

Esther closed her eyes, but not before Connie had seen her squeeze her mother's hand in response.

Eventually, Mrs Brooks turned and asked Connie, 'Is she badly hurt?'

'She has a nasty cut on her leg, but I've dressed and stitched it. I'm going to put up an antibiotic drip to prevent any infection, and I'll stay with her tonight to monitor her condition.'

Rev Brooks sighed in relief. Everyone in the room knew that Esther would have perished if she'd not been found. The Arctic and the creatures that live in that harsh environment would have shown no mercy to such a vulnerable girl.

'She was very dehydrated and cold when we found her, but I'll monitor her fluid intake and temperature through the night,' Connie added.

From the corner of her eye she could see Esther falling into a doze, exhaustion catching up with her. 'I think she needs to rest now.' Turning to Mrs Brooks, she said, 'Don't worry. I'll take good care of your girl.'

Mrs Brooks nodded, eyes brimming with tears, conflicting emotions of fear, relief, anger, and exhaustion evident in her face.

'Come on, Martha, let's get you home. Tomorrow we'll have a lot to talk about.' And her husband led her away.

Connie turned to Ilannaq. 'Thank you, Nurse Ilannaq. I think I shall call you that from now on.'

As Ilannaq opened her eyes wide in surprise and joy. Connie added, 'You go now and get some sleep. I'll need you to monitor our patient tomorrow when I rest. Even Nurse Sanders isn't superhuman.'

Ilannaq giggled and they exchanged the kind of warm hug that only close colleagues in a crisis know.

Word spread around Harbour Inlet like fire, hopping from house to house, and Daisy and Connie had apparently become the heroes of the hour. Daisy relayed all this to Connie when she returned.

'How is she doing?'

'Okay, but I just hope she doesn't get an infection. The wound looks clean enough though, and her temperature is stabilising.'

'Well, if anyone can get her through this, you can.'

Connie looked at Daisy and saw the sincerity, and yes, pride, in her eyes.

'Thank you. That means a lot.' They held each other's gaze until Daisy jumped up and grabbed her bag. 'I come armed with refreshments. I thought you would be staying here tonight so I brought sustenance.'

Connie couldn't help giggling as Daisy produced bread, tinned ham, pickles and a flask of coffee, with a flourish. 'Oh, and this...' She brandished a home-made cake in the air. 'From *maison* Brooks, believe it or not!'

'Are you sure it isn't laced with arsenic?' Connie couldn't resist the gibe.

'I think we are well past that possibility now, don't you? We are only one step away from sainthood, after all.'

'Well that's certainly new territory for me.' Connie examined the cake. 'Is that chocolate?'

'I'd put money on it, so I'll leave you get on, Nurse Sanders.' Daisy started to put her boots on.

'Why don't you stay and keep me company?' The words were out of Connie's mouth before she could stop them.

Daisy considered before she answered. 'After what happen last time you and I spent a night together? I don't think it would go down too well, do you? I think we should quit while we're flavour of the month and not put any flies in the ointment at the moment.'

She stopped at Connie's laugh. 'What?'

'How many more metaphors can you cram into that sentence?'

'Okay, but you know what I mean.'

Connie nodded reluctantly in agreement. 'You're right. This isn't the time to rock the boat.'

'Oh, a nautical theme creeping in now.'

'Off with you. I need to tend to my patient.' Connie put on her best stern-nurse voice.

Daisy saluted and was gone. Connie found herself still smiling as she checked Esther's temperature and blood pressure.

Esther's temperature started to spike the following morning. Connie left her with Ilannaq while she rushed over to the Bay to radio the Frobisher Bay medics for advice. This time, there was no teasing or any crude jokes, and the men were subdued. Connie sensed that maybe some were embarrassed by their previous cruel comments. Paul accompanied her to the radio. 'I need to ring the hospital in Frobisher Bay. I think Esther might have an infection,' she said with all the briskness she could muster.

She looked at Paul when there was no reply. After uncharacteristic shuffling of his feet, he said. 'If there is anything we...I can do to help, just tell us. I know we haven't got off to a good start and we've both said things we shouldn't have.' At this point, it was Connie's turn to look at the floor, regretting all over again her outburst at the dancing class. 'But we have to put all that behind us now. You are the professional here, and we'll support you any way we can.' It took a moment for Connie to understand this new, less arrogant Paul Archer. She looked at him and said, with real sincerity, 'Thank you, Paul.'

Striding to the radio she said, 'Right let's get some advice.'

Once Connie had described the situation, the doctor in Frobisher Bay advised that there was nothing more to be done. Connie couldn't raise the dosage of the antibiotics any further and it was just a question of waiting and hoping the infection would subside. This confirmed Connie's own thinking, but it was good to have it said by a senior medic.

Connie and Ilannaq nursed Esther while her parents sat on either side holding her hands, trying to get her to take sips of water from time to time.

'I feel so helpless,' Mrs Brooks sighed a jagged breath.

'She knows you're here and that you love her. That's all that matters,' Connie said, gently.

'I think we should pray,' said Rev Brooks, suddenly lifting his head. 'That is something we *can* do.' He looked at Connie, eyebrows raised, in an unspoken invitation for her to join them.

Connie nodded, and she and Ilannaq closed their eyes.

'Dear God, we bring before you your daughter, Esther. We pray that you will place your healing hands on her and make her well again.'

He stopped, stifling a sob. Connie squeezed his shoulder, and he took a steadying breath.

'We beseech your forgiveness for our shortcomings as parents...'

Connie opened her eyes to see Mrs Brooks lay her head on the bed, her shoulders shaking.

'Show us the way ahead. We pray that you will give Connie and Ilannaq the wisdom and strength to restore Esther to health. We put ourselves into your hands. For Jesus' sake, Amen.'

As a sea of tears was shed in the Nurse's Station, Connie knew that other members of the settlement would also be praying – each in their own way.

# Chapter Thirty

I t took five hours for the fever to break. And when Esther opened her eyes, it was as if the sun had risen on the Brooks family. There were tears, hugs, apologies and, yes, love. Connie felt it was one of the most moving things she had ever been privileged to witness, and she found herself constantly wiping tears from her eyes.

When she was able, Esther told them everything that had happened, her head bowed. 'I just felt as if I was in prison – and I had to escape. I'm sorry.' She kept her gaze on the bed. 'I know you told me to always tell you or Ilannaq when I was going there.' She looked at Connie. 'And I'm sorry but I wasn't allowed to see you, and I only saw Ilannaq with...' Esther swallowed. 'With my mother. So I couldn't.' There was silence as Esther shifted painfully to a better position, before she continued. 'I went just to think and write for a few hours, but when I got there, I slipped and my leg caught on a rock. I couldn't get up. I thought I was going to die there. That it would be punishment for my sins.' Connie could hear the tremor in Esther's voice and her heart went out to her. What sins could a thirteen-year-old girl ever commit to have to die for them?

Rev Brooks took her hand. 'We are so sorry to have made you feel that way, Esther. So sorry.'

'I just laid there, waiting to die. I don't know how long it was. Until I heard a whistle. I couldn't shout or anything, but I knew someone was coming then.' Her eyes filled with tears. 'Thank you, Connie. And thank Daisy too. I just hope I can be like you when I get older.'

Connie nodded in response, her eyes filling yet again, not daring to look at Mrs Brooks.

'I think you could do a lot worse, Esther.' Connie couldn't believe the words that Mrs Brooks had just uttered.

A few minutes later, having moved to tidy things away and update her notes, Connie whirled round as the sound of a dull *thump* sounded loud in the room. Hearing a cry from Esther, she hurried to Mrs Brooks's collapsed form on the floor.

Gently laying her on her back and noticing the bluish tinge around her lips, Connie heard a faint, fluttery heartbeat through the stethoscope which Ilannaq had handed to her before she could ask.

'What's the matter with her?' shrieked Esther. 'Connie, what's going on?'

'Esther, can you get over to that chair with Ilannaq's help? I need to get your mother on to the bed.'

Ilannaq calmed the terrified girl and, arm around her, led her to the other side of the room. 'Your mum is in good hands. Let's let Connie do her job.' She wheeled a curtain between Esther and her mother.

As she checked Mrs Brooks's pulse again, from what seemed a great distance, Connie heard Ilannaq keeping Esther talking and making her a hot drink.

'This has all been too much for her.' Rev Brooks knelt beside her clasping his wife's hand.

'Can you help me lift her on to the bed?'

Connie was surprised at how light Mrs Brooks was.

'She's not been well for a while, has she?' Connie met his gaze. 'I know she had a turn when I was with her one day.'

He nodded in acknowledgement. 'I tried to persuade her, but she refused to see you, or go to Frobisher Bay for tests. Is it her heart?'

Connie nodded. 'Yes, I think so.'

'You know, I think she's been quite frightened,' he added in a small voice. 'I should have done something.'

'Don't think about that now, the main thing is to get her stabilised. She'll need to be flown out to Frobisher Bay as soon as possible. Do you think you could organise that?'

Without speaking, he left, seemingly glad of something practical to do.

Connie's own heart almost froze in her chest as she felt the thready pulse drift to a stop, knowing she had to start chest compressions. She carried out the task which she had practised many times, but never before on a real person. She willed herself to keep calm and count the compressions carefully, thankful for the screen keeping Esther protected from the sight of her dying mother. She kept going, glancing at the clock on the wall, marking how much time had passed.

In the silence, Ilannaq put her head around the screen, her eyes wide at the scene playing out before her. Connie paused, held a finger to her lips and listened again for a heartbeat, and there it was, a faint effort from the heart to hold on to life. Connie motioned to Ilannaq to raise Mrs Brooks's head up onto a pillow and she sat, rubbing her hand, willing the heart to rally. To her relief, the unearthly bluish pallor around Mrs Brooks's lips started to fade and a stronger heartbeat was discernible.

By the time Esther peeped around the curtain, unable to bear the suspense any longer, her mother was most definitely alive. She limped to her bedside, steadied by Connie and threw her arms around her. 'Okay, let's just give your mum a bit of space for a minute,' she said, gently.

'Is she going to be alright?'

'She's going to need to go to hospital at Frobisher Bay to find out what the problem is. Once they've decided what needs to be done, I'm sure she'll be fine.' Esther didn't take her eyes off her mother.

'Your father is organising a flight, and I'm going to suggest that you go too, just for a check to make sure that your wound is okay. You and your mum are both going to need a good rest after all this.' Connie smiled and put an arm around her shoulders.

'But it's all my fault.' Esther burst into tears. Connie remembered her own utterance of exactly the same words the previous day, and how Daisy had made her see sense and shown her how to put her own feelings into a wider context.

'I don't think any of us think that, and certainly your parents don't want you to think like that. You've heard what they said. You need to be strong for them now, and nobody needs to be thinking about who's fault anything is,' Connie said firmly.

Rev Brooks appeared, ashen, in the doorway looking as if he too might collapse, but Connie saw the relief in his face that his wife and daughter were safe. 'There'll be a flight over within a few hours and I've arranged for Esther to go as well,' he added.

'Excellent, I was just suggesting the same to Esther.'

'Thank you so much, Connie.' There was genuine warmth and affection in the handshake.

As she was leaving, Mrs Brooks cleared her throat and said, 'Nurse Sanders...Connie. I know we might never be friends, but I want you to know that I'll never forget what you did for Esther and for me. I can never condone what you...whatever it is, but I should never have let my religious bias cloud my judgement of you as a person – or Daisy for that matter. And I agree with Esther, she couldn't have a better role model than you.' And as she was making her way out of the door, helped by her husband, to the waiting Hudson Bay vehicle, she spoke without turning around. 'I'm sure you'll get over this faze and marry a nice young man one of these days.'

Connie gave an inward sigh, but the adult Connie was gracious. 'Thank you, Mrs Brooks. I appreciate that.' She was still pondering on the new-but-still-somehow-the-same Mrs Brooks when Daisy appeared.

'Are you all right, Connie?' Daisy draped an arm around Connie's shoulders and looked her in the eye. 'I've just seen your patients safely headed for the Otter, so you can relax now and have a well-earned break.'

Daisy's blonde hair, the concerned blue eyes and the weight of her arm on Connie's shoulder took her breath away but at the same time made her feel weak under the weight of it, as if she wasn't strong enough to bear it. She shifted slightly, causing Daisy to move away.

Connie immediately berated herself. What was wrong with her? Why couldn't she admit how she felt? What made her keep denying it and distancing herself from the very thing she wanted? Deep down, she knew the answer – fear. Familiar fear of Daisy turning into another Helen. She couldn't go back to that heartbreak again. But there was also another fear. Fear of what people would say if she allowed her feelings for Daisy to show.

'You look like you're about to keel over. Come on let's get you something to eat.'

Connie glanced at the discarded chocolate cake, still untouched in its box.

'Yup. I think you could definitely do with some of that.' Daisy grabbed the box and tucked it under her arm.

'I'm so tired but I'm not ready for bed,' Connie found herself saying, after hot chocolate and several pieces of cake had been consumed.

As soon as they were both settled with a whisky each, sitting on Connie's settee with their feet tucked under them, Daisy looked at her and said, 'Right, spill! What is going on, Connie Sanders?'

Connie remained silent, not knowing where to start.

'Look, Connie, I know something is going on. Even though we've been getting along...there's still something, isn't there? Is it me? Have I made you uncomfortable? Because that's the last thing I would ever want.'

Connie was devastated. She knew now, whether she wanted to or not, that she loved this woman and the last thing she wanted to do was to hurt her – she hadn't realised that her thoughts had been so obvious to anyone but herself, and more important, hadn't realised that Daisy had cared so much.

'I can't do this, Connie. If I've done something, then tell me – that's the least you can do! We're friends and I care about you.'

Connie got up and walked to the kitchen to pour another coffee. She had made a mess of everything...again! This had not been supposed to happen. Coming to the Arctic should have been the start of a better, more honest, life. If she was not honest with Daisy, she would lose her friendship anyway – which would be the final blow to her Arctic adventure. 'Connie Sanders, get over there and tell this woman how you feel. Start as you mean to go on,' she told herself sternly. 'Where is your adventurer spirit?'

She took a breath, picked up her fresh coffee and sat down close to Daisy, taking her hand. 'Okay, this is a first for me, so hang on in there. Daisy, you are the most wonderful, funny, beautiful, intelligent... I could go on...woman I have ever met, and...' Connie gulped in a breath of air, 'I think I care about you...and not just as a friend,' she added. 'But I don't know what to do, or what that means...' her voice trailed away.

Daisy looked into her eyes and Connie felt her insides melt as she held her breath.

'Connie, it's you who are brave, beautiful, mad, and... I could go on. I had no idea you felt that way. You've done a damn good job at hiding it! It never occurred to me that this could really happen, even though it's what I've wanted – more than anything. I think I've always known, ever since we met, that I feel the same way about you, even though, like you, I couldn't even say it to myself. We've both been running from our pasts, afraid to move forward in case something else, something worse happens. But maybe now is the time for some of your grandfather's adventurer courage. Time for us to take a step of trust and move forwards together.'

Connie turned and took Daisy into her arms and held her tight. She was never, never going to let this woman go, even if she had to walk over coals to be by her side.

They looked into each other's eyes, and Daisy suddenly burst into peals of laughter. 'Oh my God! Someone up there must be raising their eyes to the heavens and saying, "At last! Those two are something else."'

'Yes, we are something else – in lots of ways.' Connie laughed and felt all the broken pieces inside her start to re-form into a new, braver, more honest Connie.

She took Daisy's face in her hands and kissed her gently. 'This is how something else we are!'

# Chapter Thirty-One

E arly summer in the Arctic was a combination of the bluest skies and warm days, and a constant battle with the mosquitos. Connie fought off a swarm of these annoying insects as she tried to adjust her position in the kayak without toppling over into the still-icy waters of Hudson Bay – even in summer, cold enough to kill anyone who fell overboard or missed their footing jumping from one ice floe to another near the floe edge.

She watched Daisy's back, her blonde curls bouncing over powerful shoulders as she paddled, and felt a wave of warmth and affection wash over her. Was Connie Saunders the luckiest girl – no, not girl – woman, in the whole world? Here she was in one of the most spectacular places on earth with someone who cared about her, just as she was. Unlike Helen, Daisy didn't give Connie the unsustainable illusion that she was the centre of her world, but she gave something different, something more solid and lasting. And she respected Connie – that was also a new experience, although Connie had had to work hard to earn that respect. It was not something given easily, as Patty had told Connie on their latest conversation.

As if reading her thoughts, Daisy turned and smiled. 'Nearly at the floe edge. How are your arms holding up?'

Connie, lost in her thoughts hadn't noticed her aching arms until now. 'I think they'll manage,' she said waving the paddle in the air.

Daisy had assured her that there were always plenty of seals where the ice met the sea, as they came at this time to give birth to their pups on the ice floes, and Connie had made sure to bring her camera and several rolls of film.

'Look, there!' Daisy pointed, and Connie could just make out a white furry blob on one of the ice sheets.

'Oh my goodness. Is that...?'

'The cutest little baby seal ever? Probably.'

They paddled silently until they were near enough for Connie to capture the moment on film. As she looked through the viewfinder, a pair of large, black eyes stared at her, the seal tipping its head to one side in a questioning gesture. She pressed the shutter a few times and put the camera in her lap, content to just look until there was a sudden splash as the mother appeared, awkwardly climbing on to the ice with food for her young,

Connie and Daisy spent an hour or so paddling between the ice floes until they reached the point where the melting sea met the white land. There they beached the kayak and shared a meal of bannock, blueberry buns and a flask of coffee, all the while fighting off the mosquitos.

'I don't think I'll ever forget this day.' Connie leaned against Daisy's shoulder. 'I want to soak up every single moment, so that I can remember it when I'm old. Remember that I...we, did this. I want to have stories to tell when I'm old. I want to have done things.'

Daisy put an arm around her. 'I think you've already got quite a few stories to tell, and you're only twenty-two. And if I know anything about Connie Sanders, there will be many more. I know it's early days, but I'm living my best life, here with you, too.'

'It's weird to think that this time tomorrow you'll be back in Frobisher Bay.' Connie looked out over the bay and sighed. 'I'll miss you.'

'Ah, but this time you know that I'll miss you too, and it'll only be a month before you join me.'

Connie smiled. 'I know, I can't believe that I'm actually going to see roads and cars and lots of people.' She paused. 'And it's amazing that they think I'm responsible enough to actually train anyone!'

'Well, you'd better believe it, because there will be two little student nurses hanging on your every word.'

Connie marvelled that Harbour Inlet was to be a training base for nurses from overseas who, like her had escaped to the Arctic, for whatever reason. Her suggestion, with a supporting letter from Rev Brooks had persuaded the authorities that it was not acceptable to throw nurses in the deep end as she had been, and that some on-site training was needed in advance of their postings. Ilannaq was due to start her training at the end of the summer but would hold the fort while Connie was preparing the training course in Frobisher Bay, at which point Connie would return with her two students. Patty had been consulted and was also part of the new arrangement, and Connie couldn't wait to meet her radio friend face-to-face.

'I think we should move before we get eaten alive,' said Daisy, standing and waving the mosquitos away.

Connie had put her hands on the ground to lever herself up, when she sensed Daisy freeze. Following her gaze, Connie caught her breath as a magnificent polar bear ambled along the floe edge with two cubs. They were around a hundred yards away, downwind.

Daisy slowly lowered herself to the ground, instinctively reaching for the nearby gun, but the bear was seemingly too busy with her cubs to notice. She nudged them into the water, before walking in herself and swimming around them. The cubs were hesitant, but eventually one of them lost its footing and found itself swimming. Within minutes it was revelling in the newfound sense of freedom and the playground that was the water, soon joined by its sibling. In spite of the creeping cold, Connie and Daisy stayed still, until the mother bear eventually came out of the water and shook herself dry, followed by the cubs. And for a heart-stopping minute or two, she looked in their direction, as if sensing their presence. And for those few precious minutes, the world stopped for Connie. Then, she ambled away, followed by her cubs, blending into the white landscape, and disappearing. 'Thank you, *Nanuk*.' Connie breathed. She clasped Daisy's hand, tears in her eyes.

'You are such a romantic, Connie Sanders!' Daisy pulled her to her feet. 'Come on, we don't want you getting frostbite again.'

Once they were safely back in the relative warmth of the kayak, Daisy and Connie headed back to Harbour Inlet, and humans. Now she was a real adventurer – she hoped her grandfather was watching.

# Chapter Thirty-Two

The following morning was full of bustle, as Daisy, along with Kathy and Tom prepared to leave. Oliver was also being relocated to another Hudson Bay depot. He gave Connie a long, departing hug.

'Take care, Connie...and thank you.'

'For what?' She held him at arm's length.

'For understanding.'

She nodded, seeing the tears in his eyes.

'Get going, before you start me off, you idiot.' Connie punched his arm playfully. 'I hope we can keep in touch,' she called as he headed for the kayak. He waved over his shoulder without turning around.

Kathy and Tom were surrounded by a crowd of well-wishers, and there were many jokes about their long summer holidays. Kathy hugged Connie. 'Take care, Nurse Sanders. Keep on being gutsy – it suits you.' Just as she was walking away, Kathy stopped and turned. 'And please can you tell Elizabeth not to use all the butter this summer!'

Connie laughed. 'I'll do my best. But I can't guarantee she'll listen.'

The moment came for Connie to leave. They had said their goodbyes in private last night, but neither hesitated to give the other a long, unflinching hug. They turned, surprised at the ripple of applause that ran through the bystanders, led by Ilannaq and Moosasee and their family. And looking at each other, they smiled and touched foreheads before Daisy tore herself away.

It was a day of mixed emotions, because as well as departures there were exciting arrivals. Elizabeth, Peter and Tom could be seen approaching slowly and surely as the paddlers brought them towards the shore, Tom waving excitedly. Connie looked up as the Otter rose into the sky and circled above them. As she waved, watching it disappear into the distance, Connie sensed arms around her legs and looked down to see Tom, who seemed to have grown from a toddler to a sturdy little boy in no time.

'Hello, stranger,' she said stooping to return the hug.

'I saw Esther,' he said, importantly.

'Oh wow! That's good. How is she?'

'She's alright, but she's going to a school in England where you stay all night.' Tom frowned disapprovingly.

'I can tell you, she's looking forward to it, though.' Connie's heart leapt at the familiar voice and looked up to see Elizabeth, who enveloped her in a hug, as strong and sturdy as ever.

'Ohhh, I am so pleased to see you!' Connie gasped as the air was squeezed out of her lungs.

'You look different, Connie.' Elizabeth, stood back, appraising her. 'Somehow, my Arctic daughter has grown up while I've been away.'

'I think you may be right. I've so much to tell you, Elizabeth.'

Peter approached. 'Well hello, my star photography student. I've seen your work in the gallery in Montreal – not bad.' He gave her a hug. 'I've taught you well, even though I say so myself!'

'Come on, big-head, we've got sorting and unpacking to do.' Elizabeth clapped him on his back, rolling her eyes at Connie.

'Coffee later?' she called over her shoulder as they headed up the beach.

'Of course.' Connie shouted in reply.

Elizabeth nodded in approval at Connie's sponge cake. 'Very good. I'm impressed.'

'I have to say I've had a few tips from François. She makes the most amazing pastries,' Connie replied.

'So I've heard. News has travelled through the Hudson Bay community and there is some envy of the Harbour Inlet bakery section.' Elizabeth finished a final mouthful and brushed the crumbs from her sweater. 'And talking of news travelling, I've heard about your adventures and life-saving activities. Mrs Brooks is doing well after her heart surgery and is going back to England with Esther. I think she's planning on staying with her sister who lives near the school, while Esther settles in.'

'I'm glad Esther is going to get to live the life she deserves. I've worried about her.'

'She's so looking forward to going back to England, and when we saw her in Frobisher Bay, she was like a different girl from the Esther I used to know. And I know that part of that is down to you.'

Connie answered ruefully, 'I didn't always get it right, though.'

'But who does? Life is tricky, and if you're living it to the full, you'll always have enemies of one sort or another. And it seems to me that you've learnt to choose which battles to fight and which aren't worth the effort, or even yours to fight.' Elizabeth sat back, putting her hands behind her head and stretched. 'And you've stopped running,' she said, almost as an afterthought.

Connie considered, and realised with amazement that, yes, she *had* stopped running – without realising it. She was no longer that frightened, angry girl who had arrived on the Otter a year ago, running blindly from pain and humiliation, consumed by fear of not being included or accepted for who she was, and naïvely thinking that people on the other side of the world would be different. And the woman sitting next to her had set her on this path and encouraged her to stay the course. She turned to Elizabeth and hugged her close. 'I couldn't have done it without you,' she murmured, her voice muffled by Elizabeth's jumper.

After a few moments, Elizabeth sat back and studied Connie. 'I think you would have, you know. I always sensed you were a survivor and a fighter.' She paused, looking out of the window as if searching for the right words. 'It's you who has got yourself here, Connie. With maybe a little nudge here and there from me, Ilannaq, and your other friends.' She looked at Connie. 'I'm so proud of my Arctic daughter.'

Tears prickled in Connie's eyes at the affection in Elizabeth's voice, and she thought of her real mother who had never been able to articulate any love for her daughter. But she had written that one sentence, and every time Connie looked at the moon, she thought of her mother, far away, on another continent, thinking of her daughter. She had cared but had never known how to show it. With thoughts of home, the realisation suddenly dawned on Connie that the prospect of going back to her old life in Manchester was unthinkable now, a year on. She could not un-experience her life in the Arctic, and there was no going back to the old Connie.

Lost in her thoughts, Connie realised that Elizabeth was saying something. 'And now you have Daisy. I'm so glad you found the courage to let someone into your heart. Someone who you'll be safe with and who will love you in the way you deserve. All I want is for my girl to be happy.'

This time, there was no way to stop the tears as they flowed down Connie's cheeks.

# Epilogue

C onnie closed the journal and leant her head back against the chair, closing her eyes.

'Are you okay, Aunt Connie?'

She turned her head and smiled at her great-niece. 'Yes, I'm fine, Katy,' she said. 'But reliving one's life at this age can be almost more tiring than living it the first time round.'

'I think you and Aunt Daisy are so cool!' Connie felt Katy's hand in hers. 'And to think that you worried about not having stories to tell when you got old... Older,' she corrected herself hastily.

At seventy-five, Connie guessed she must seem ancient to her fifteen-year-old great-niece. In some ways she reminded her of Esther, but in other ways she was very different. Katy was a confident girl with lots of friends, and her parents had never stopped showing her how much she was loved, and how special she was. But not in a cloying way, Katy would never have tolerated that. Even at fifteen, she was already her own woman.

As if reading her thoughts, Katy asked, 'What happened to Esther? I feel so sorry for her. I would have hated her life!'

'After the accident, and once she was settled in at her new school, Esther blossomed into an amazing young woman. The school encouraged her writing talent, as did her parents, once they got over their religious scruples. They were never going to let those get in the way of their relationship with their daughter again.'

'So did she become a writer?'

'After many years of teaching English. Have you heard of E.M. Brooks?'

Katy gasped, her hand over her mouth. 'What! E.M. Brooks is Esther?'

Connie nodded.

'OMG, she is amazing! We've read *White Wilderness* in school. I can't believe you know her.'

'We've kept in touch, and she comes to see me from time to time when she's over here. She comes more often now that her parents have died. I think they enjoyed their retirement in that little cottage in the cathedral close. Mrs Brooks always wanted to get back to Winchester... Anyway, to get back to Esther, I think her next book is going to be about horses. Something like *Black Beauty*.'

'The very first book you leant her!' Katy said breathlessly. 'And does she know about your photography, all your awards?'

'Yes, she does, and we are mutually proud of each other.' Connie smiled.

'What about you? Was it hard to give up nursing to do photography?'

'Not really. Once Daisy and I settled in Montreal, it was time for a change. I did enjoy my years in Frobisher Bay, setting up the training scheme though. And I was so proud when Ilannaq qualified. She never let anyone forget that she was the first Inuit nurse in her area, and Harbour Inlet was in good hands under her care. Aunt Daisy encouraged me to give professional photography a go. I don't think I'd have had the courage without her support.'

'You and Aunt Daisy were so brave – so *out there* for those days.'

'We had to be discreet sometimes, but eventually everyone seemed to get used to the fact that we were an item.'

'I mean "out" as in gay, but also "out there" as in...' Katy searched for the word. 'Pioneers. We'd call you "influencers" now, maybe. But I don't know of any YouTube or TikTok influencers that have done anything remotely in your league! You and Aunt Daisy did things that not many women did back then. Esther was right about you being a role model.'

Connie nodded. 'I guess so. When we eventually got married, it was a miracle. We could never have imagined that happening, even in our wildest dreams, back in the seventies.'

'It's so different now. Loads of kids at school have come out – it's almost boring to be straight these days, like me.' Katy patted her chest and rolled her eyes.

Connie could never get over her amazement at how Katy's generation were able to talk about sexuality with so much openness. She thought back to her conversation with Oliver, where they had reached an understanding about their sexuality, but had not had the language or confidence to talk about it openly. She had lost touch after he had left Harbour Inlet, but Connie hoped he met someone worthy of him, and that he had had had a good life.

'But going back to the wedding,' Katy reminded her. 'That was an amazing day. I can still remember it. Anyone can see how much you and Aunt Daisy still love each other, even after all this time. I wish I had known all this back then, and maybe I could have put names to faces. But I do remember Lady Katherine though, she was so nice, even though her husband was a bit weird. Only you and Aunt Daisy could have had British aristocracy at your wedding!'

Connie had long since stopped thinking of Kathy as Lady Katherine, and smiled. Katy, oblivious, hesitated for a moment. 'Was Ilannaq there?'

Connie felt tears gathering in her eyes. 'No. Ilannaq died of TB about thirty years ago.'

Katy squeezed her hand. 'That's terrible. Oh, I'm so sorry, Aunt Connie.'

'You would have got on well with her. She was always happy and ready for a joke. Except for the one time she felt I was letting her and her community down. She didn't hesitate to tell me what she thought about that!'

'It sounds like she played quite a big part in getting you and Aunt Daisy together.' Katy gave a mischievous smile. 'A kind of Arctic Cupid.'

I'd never quite thought of Ilannaq like that, and now I'll never get that image out of my head! Thanks for that, Katy!'

Katy laughed. 'But seriously, I'd love to go up north and see Frobisher Bay and Harbour Inlet, maybe I could get Mum and Dad to take me, or even Grandpa. Maybe I could persuade him to go on a painting expedition.'

'I don't think I'd recognise Frobisher Bay now. Iqaluit, as it's now called, is a big, modern city. Many of the Inuit live and work there and have left behind their culture to live very different lives. You would never see the Frobisher Bay I saw. And with global warming, the sea ice is disappearing, so the Inuit life is changing, even for those still living in settlements. It was already starting to change when I was there. But, on the plus side – because it's not all doom and gloom – Harbour Inlet now has its own airstrip and all the amenities you can think of. Lots of my Inuit friends are on Facebook, so I can keep in touch.'

'What do you think about the Western influence on the Inuit, now that you're not a radical youngster anymore?'

Connie smiled and then sighed and thought. What did she think? 'There are lots of things I'm not happy about, such as the loss of the Inuit culture and way of life. And I'm aware of my part in that, as a Westerner. But in other ways, I have to remember what Ilannaq said; that her people couldn't live without being part of the developing world. She embraced a lot of the changes, and the communities have a much better healthcare system now – something that was practically non-existent when I first went to Harbour Inlet. Also, the Inuit are represented in politics and on local councils, and are an integral part of the decision-making process. Many have benefitted from a better education and have trained to be doctors and lawyers and other skilled professionals. So, all in all, I guess it is what it is. Some positives and some negatives. But it is absolutely right that the appalling things the Canadian government did to the Inuit in the twentieth century are now out in the open.' Connie felt a flicker of her old fiery spirit. She closed her eyes for a moment, briefly revisiting her twenty-one-year-old self, before continuing. 'It's easy to be sentimental about the past, but even so, I'm not sure that the Inuit are any happier now than they were living their old, traditional way of life. Some, like Moosasee's grandson are setting up training hubs to teach the younger generation the traditional skills of their ancestors, and to make them proud of their heritage. That's got to be a good thing.' Connie looked at Katy, listening with rapt attention and admired her passion and interest. 'Sorry, that was a bit of a long, convoluted answer, Katy, but I guess there is no, one, simple answer to a question like that.'

'I'm trying to do my bit to fight global warming. Do you remember when we all walked out of school on Fridays a few years ago? Greta Thunberg is right up there, along with you and Aunt Daisy. But things are not looking good, especially for life in the Arctic. We, the next generation will have to keep fighting.'

'And you will. You have a warrior spirit. It runs in the family.'

Connie, feeling that she needed to move around a bit after reliving the past, stood up. 'Shall we have a walk around the garden, before a cup of tea?'

'Sounds good. Grandpa should be here in about half an hour.' Katy jumped to her feet, and Connie felt a moment of envy at her youthful energy.

As they strolled around hers and Daisy's Montreal garden, Connie, as always, stopped to admire and smell the flowers. She had never got over the novelty of the roses and sweet peas she lovingly tended. The trees cast a welcome shadow over the summer heat, and she wondered how she had lived for all that time without experiencing these wonderful living things. But, she reminded herself, she had seen many other, equally wonderful things that most people would never experience.

'When is Aunt Daisy back?' Katy broke into her thoughts.

'Any day now. You know Aunt Daisy, she's never likes being cooped up in one place for too long. Definitely still a free spirit.'

'Is she still in the north?'

'Yes, in Yellowknife. She couldn't resist an invitation to take part in some research on the Dene people. I don't think she'll ever retire.'

'But don't you miss her?'

'Of course I do, but it makes it all the more special when she comes home. Relationships are all about setting each other free and letting the one you love fly. If anyone doesn't encourage you to do that, they're not right for you.' Connie turned to Katy. 'Don't ever forget that. Freedom is what keeps a relationship strong.'

Katy nodded and kissed Connie's cheek, just as the sound of approaching footsteps could be heard along the path.

Connie raised her arms in welcome as David appeared and took her into his arms, giving her a bear hug. 'How is my favourite sister?' he said, releasing her and placing her arm through his.

'She's your only sister, Grandad!' They all laughed at the well-worn joke.

'Great-aunt Connie has been telling me her life story.' Katy bounced on her toes in excitement.

'What, *all* of it?' her grandfather affected pretend incredulity.

Connie squeezed his arm. Since Carla, David's wife had died, he had spent more and more time with Daisy and Connie in Canada, until the day came when it had seemed the obvious thing to move there. She loved knowing that he was only a few streets away, and could imagine him pottering around in his studio at all times of the day and night.

'I hope my granddaughter hasn't been plying you with too many questions,' he said. 'I know she has a tendency to ask a lot.' He winked at Connie.

'I'll leave you two to it and make some tea.' Katy gave them a fond look that suddenly made Connie feel rather old.

'There's cake in the tin on the table,' Connie called after her.

As she and David resumed their walk, she asked, 'Are you enjoying having Katy over for the summer?'

'She's like a breath of fresh air. But I'd forgotten young people have so much energy,' he replied. 'I'm so glad you've shared your story with her. She already thinks you and Daisy are wonderful, but I think it's important that she knows that it's not always been easy.'

'No. Our parents were very different to the parents of today, weren't they? But they did what they thought was right and only wanted the best for us. Do you regret being a lawyer and not a painter?'

'Not really. I hate to admit it, but I think they did have a point about having a sensible career. I don't think I'm really the starving-artist-in-the-garret material. But I'm loving it now that I have time, and don't have to worry about where the next penny is coming from.' He stopped to smell a rose, inhaling deeply. 'Roses always remind me of Dad, do you remember that awful horse manure he used to put on them?' They chuckled, sharing the memory. 'They did miss you, you know. When you went.' David was suddenly serious.

'Did they?' Connie asked, although she already knew the truth, deep down.

'They never said much. But I know they read your letters over and over again.' Connie's eyes filled with tears as she recalled her youthful thoughtlessness, and was glad that she'd gone to visit them with Daisy. Her father and Daisy had really hit it off, and when her parents agreed to come over to Canada to visit, she could hardly believe it. Connie was grateful for those times.

'Changing the subject, how is the indomitable Elizabeth?'

'She found it hard after Peter died, but spends a lot of time with Tom and his children in Vancouver. I think she's a great-grandmother now. Still visits the north regularly though. She knows so many people, she's never short of somewhere to stay.' They walked a few more paces.

'I'm beginning to think this tea will never materialise. I'll go and see what Katy is up to. Why don't you wait here.' He indicated Connie's favourite bench. 'I'll make sure she isn't wrecking your kitchen and give you a shout when it's ready.' David patted her hand, before heading back to the house.

Connie sat back looking at the same clear blue sky she had seen on those early days in the Arctic. It was a long time since she had gone back over her journals, and reliving her time in Harbour Inlet had brought many mixed, emotions to the surface. She thought about Katy with her life ahead of her and hoped she would value those all-too-brief years of youth and vigour. For Connie they seemed to have passed in a flash. But she had achieved her goal of having stories to tell when she was older and felt that she had lived her life to the full, and maybe done some good along the way. The gift of her relationship with Daisy had enabled her to do so much more than she would have achieved on her own, she was sure of that. Closing her eyes, she thought of the Inuit view of the cycle of life and death, and their calm, dignified acceptance of it. It was time to hand over to the next generation to carry on, and if they were anything like Katy, she felt the world would be in good hands.

# Acknowledgements

My thanks to Glen for reading and checking the book through, several times! Also big thank-yous to my fabulous beta readers. As ever, another brilliant cover design. Thank you Kostis.

# About Sheena

Sheena has always been an avid reader of anything and everything, and is a firm believer that you can never have too many books. Although she loved her previous career as a music teacher, she is now enjoying life as a fiction editor and, lately, a writer. The everyday has always fascinated Sheena and much of her writing is based on snippets of conversations overheard in cafes, shops or anywhere that people are together. She aims for writing that is a blend of observational humour (think Victoria Wood or Peter Kay) and emotionally challenging situations for her characters to deal with, all within the context of a good story. She lives in Nottinghamshire.

If you would like to read more tales like this, **Shifting Horizons**, Sheena's book of short stories and flash fiction is available on Amazon. To find out more and sign up to Sheena's mailing list to get exclusive access to new material, go to https://sheenabillettauthor.com

If you enjoyed **From Manchester to the Arctic**, I would love it if you could leave a review on Amazon or Goodreads, or both! Thank you, Sheena :)

# Coming Soon

Vanstone Press is pleased to announce **The Woman Who Wrote in Green Ink**, Sheena's next book, coming later in 2023.

Finding a set of journals and diaries in an antique shop, all written in green ink, leads to unexpected consequences for Amber.

Sign up at https://sheenabillettauthor.com to keep updated with Sheena's writing and to see Kostis's cover design for **The Woman Who Wrote in Green Ink**, coming soon.

Printed in Great Britain
by Amazon

19678585R00141